Call Me Ringo

The man called Ringo almost drowned in a flooded river, but thanks to a strange old wanderer calling himself Cap he survived.

Ringo was a man who didn't care to be beholden to anyone. So when Cap told him about his quest for vengeance, Ringo knew how he could square the score. What he didn't know was just how much blood and gunsmoke he was riding into. And he began to have doubts about the man to whom he owed his life.

Who was he? Could he be trusted? Now it was a case of life or death – Ringo's.

By the same author

Shoot on Sight
Hellfire Pass
Blood Kin
The Cougar Canyon Run
Travis Quinn, Outlaw
Bronco Madigan
Cimarron Arrow
Madigan's Star
Count Your Bullets
Madigan's Lady
Bull's-Eye
Madigan's Sidekick
Tennessee Renegade
Graveyard Gold
Madigan's Mistake
Nevada Hawk
Find Madigan!
Both Sides of the Law
Once a Ranger

Call Me Ringo

Hank J. Kirby

A Black Horse Western

ROBERT HALE · LONDON

© Hank J. Kirby 2008
First published in Great Britain 2008

ISBN 978-0-7090-8531-7

Robert Hale Limited
Clerkenwell House
Clerkenwell Green
London EC1R 0HT

www.halebooks.com

Typeset by
Derek Doyle & Associates, Shaw Heath
Printed and bound in Great Britain by
Antony Rowe Limited, Wiltshire

PROLOGUE

SATISFACTION

'That, sir, is a damned lie! I demand an instant apology!'

Looking into the outraged face of the young captain in his neat dress uniform, the middle-aged man in coat tails and flowered vest curled a lip. 'You can go to hell – sir!'

'Then – I demand satisfaction.'

The captain stepped forward and, taking one of his issue leather gauntlets from where it was folded under his white leather belt, whipped it across the pinched face of the civilian. The blow had considerable force and the man staggered, unwanted tears of pain filling his dark eye cavities. Two of his group steadied him and many of the guests at this fund-raising musical recital, *Songs Of The South – Remembered,* turned towards the corner where the small drama was being enacted.

The captain glanced at the uniformed man beside

him. 'You'll oblige me by acting as my second, Lieutenant?'

The man swallowed, straightened ramrod stiff and bowed his head. 'I would be honoured, sir.'

The captain glared coldly at the civilian who was still being steadied by one of his friends, his face bearing the rapidly reddening mark of the gauntlet.

'Make the arrangements!' the captain snapped, turned and strode nonchalantly through the stunned silence now hanging over the crowded ballroom.

The mist on the naked sandbar was almost luminous in the pale glare of the still unseen sun. The river flowed on as it had done for centuries, untouched by the closeness of death about to arrive on the small island.

Two skiffs were drawn up on the gravelly beach. Shadowy figures threw distorted shapes through the mists as men went about their grim business. Voices were low but curt, orders given, obeyed in tense silence.

The captain seemed at ease, allowing the lieutenant to take his heavy coat, rolling the sleeves of his white cotton shirt back to halfway between wrists and elbows. He shivered slightly and the lieutenant cleared his throat, spoke in a low voice.

'Sir, it is my duty to remind you, even at this late stage, that it is against army regulations to participate in a duel. The penalties are severe, long prison sentences, even death, if it should be judged as murder.'

'Proceed, Lieutenant,' the captain said quietly,

voice steady and clear. 'I am well aware of army regulations.'

'If he were to make an apology. . . ? Would you
accept, sir, and call off this very dangerous proceed-
ing?'

The captain strained to see the narrow face, scared
white, but the man still eager to please. 'If the apology were to be made in public, before all who heard
the insult – I might reconsider.'

There was a flurry of movement as the lieutenant
went to meet the civilian's seconds and conveyed the
captain's offer. He returned slowly, face wooden.

'He will apologize, sir – here and now, man to
man, but not in public.'

The captain's gaze was steady. 'Then bring the
pistols and let us get on with it.'

There was no further delay. The duelling pistols
were brought in their polished cherrywood box,
offered for selection, exquisite examples of the
gunsmith's trade, from Pommeroy and Mitchum in
Pennsylvania. Octagonal, rifled barrels – one of the
first such barrels on duelling pistols – foresights
carved from ivory chips so as to be more readily visible, triggers finely set on expertly tempered blued-
steel springs, even the wonderfully symmetrical butts
with their *fleur*-shaped caps had been contoured to
take a man's fingers in hand-worked ridges, for
comfort and the chance of better accuracy. Each
powder load, carefully measured and weighed, was
wrapped in combustible paper, the projectiles hand-
cast, sanded to smoothness and accurate bore size.

Beautiful and efficient death, awaiting release. . . .

The selection was made carelessly by the civilian: what was there to choose between such weapons? The captain hefted his pistol, handed it to the lieutenant who, like the civilian's assistant, began to load carefully, though the army man's hands shook slightly.

The blank-faced officious surgeon laid out his gleaming instruments on a folding table, saws, knives, tweezers, ligatures, and pulled out his watch, which he strained to see. He spoke quietly to his assistant.

'Damn mist – they'll both need cat's eyes to find target.'

Then the seconds, bustling, stood the men back to back, stepped away and at a nod from the lieutenant, a man whose lower face was covered with a dark bandanna, began to count in a strong voice, '*One – two – three. . . .*'

The captain and the civilian moved apart to the slow cadence, arms bent, pistol barrels vertical alongside their taut faces, blued-steel hammers at full cock.

'– nine – ten. Halt – turn – present.'

The men obeyed, faced each other, twenty paces apart, already sighting down the damp planes of the barrel tops. The ivory tips were clearly visible through the shrouding mist as they settled steadily on target.

The world seemed to stand still, pause in its eternal spinning. Silence fell over the sandbar. Even the river seemed hushed. Breaths were drawn in – held.

'*Fire at your leisure, gentlemen!*'

The pistols' reports sounded as one, long daggers

of flame leaping from the muzzles, clouds of powder-smoke swirling and blending with the mist, adding their opaqueness to the scene.

There was a muffled grunt, a shuffling sound as a body fell.

The surgeon hurried forward, snapping at the seconds and the survivor to stand back while he saw to the loser. He turned to glance up at the victor. 'You are a fine shot, Captain. The ball took your opponent squarely through the heart. I must—'

Then the hazy shape of the captain swayed, the heavy pistol fell from his hand, and he collapsed on top of it, his spurting blood staining the polished cherrywood and gleaming metal-work before spilling off to soak into the gravel of the sandbar.

CHAPTER 1

A HELLUVA WAY
TO DIE

The river boiled around the black horse's chest and the lower legs of the rider lying forward, clinging tightly to reins and saddlehorn. Creamy foam surged up and into his gaunt face. He coughed, reared up drunkenly, spitting.

Too distressed to see clearly, he thought there was a pink tinge to the saliva.

Blood – his blood – bullet must've gone deeper than he thought. A thrill of fear sent a wave of goosebumps over his aching body. Must've clipped a lung. . . .

He felt himself slipping sideways out of the saddle, clamped his fingers around the horn more tightly, twisted the rein ends around his other wrist.

But he had little strength and knew he was done for. The damn river was in flood. And no wonder – this country hadn't seen rain like the downpours of the last week in a coon's age. Why, back there, some-where over his left shoulder, he had seen an entire house washed up on a bend, clapboards and shingles splintered and ripped away – enough so he could see the sodden bodies of a whole family inside amongst the wrecked and piled furniture. Looked like mother and father and at least two children. He would remember the way the little girl's golden hair waved and undulated in the slopping muddy water for as long as he lived ... *which may not be for long!*

He was already carrying Carnevan's bullet, so was unable to even check if anyone was still alive in the shattered house. He knew instinctively it was hope-less, but it kept nagging: what if there had still been a breath or two in one of them? *One of the chil-dren. . . ?*

No use worrying about it now.

His boots had slipped the stirrups and his legs washed out in the current, lifting his upper body away from the saddle. The black was thrashing now, eyes rolling, head tossing wildly: the river was pound-ing it relentlessly and his vision was fading. There was a blur to his right, but nothing to his left except a vista of raging, mad waters. He was hanging to the horn now, by one hand, the reins somehow having slipped over his wet wrist.

A little bit of luck – maybe! He was hanging off the right side of the horse, closer to that blur – and if it was the small island he wanted – no longer just a sandbar after all these years – well, it was better than he expected.

Then he had no choice: the horse went under and

11

rose whickering and thrashing crazily, the violent motions wrenching his hand off the saddlehorn. The black plunged away, out of reach. In a moment he was fighting the river alone. No, fighting wasn't the word, he was too weak for that.

The river had him entirely in its power.

He lost sight of the horse. He lost sight of the world! Sucked down, buffeted and twisted and rolled, bounced along the bottom with moving stones battering his already weakened body. Lungs burned, ready to burst. His senses spun, his brain about to explode.

A helluva way to die! And so close to—

Something crashed into his legs, tumbling him even more. His groping hands felt gravel, pebbles. He gripped madly – why he didn't know, for they were loose and afforded him no help. Just more ballast to hold him down.

A freak current turned him tail over tip, kicking his legs up and over, his face scraping the river bottom, muddy water pouring down his throat. *This was it then – Like hell!*

Where that last thought came from he neither knew nor cared and wasn't even aware that he was now fighting back, losing blood but to hell with that: the river could have his blood as long as he got some air – just a mouthful – a spoonful – a breath brushing his nostrils – anything!

The light changed from murky brown to murky paleness. Coughing, retching, gagging, his reeling senses noted his head was above water now. Something slapped right down in front of his face, skimming his head, slithering over his skin. *Cottonmouth!* his brain screamed and he feebly lifted an arm to ward off the snake's strike. But no fangs lunged against his neck or face, though something curled tightly around his arm, almost wrenching it out of its socket.

He was being pulled against the current, his arm now above his head, shoulder screaming with burning pain at the joint. Something like wire cut deeply into his triceps muscle.

Not wire – rope!

That was his last conscious thought before total blackness closed down and his body went limp, sinking again.

The rain had stopped, or eased to a mere drizzle. That was his first thought. There was a steady drip-drip-drip close by and when he tentatively opened his eyes he saw an amber glow trying to push back the black cloak of night. At the same time he realized he was in some sort of brush shelter on solid ground, and it was the drizzle seeping through that dripped monotonously so close to his head.

It was hard to breathe. His chest felt as if he had an iron band slowly tightening each time he gagged for a breath. Under his left shoulder hurt as if someone was holding a branding iron, not only against his skin, but plunging it in deep. He could have struck a match on his tongue it was so dry and rough – if he could find the effort to do so. He didn't recall ever feeling so weak.

Finally his mind acknowledged his right arm. It

felt like it had been fed through Mrs McGillacuddy's mangle or crushed in a vice. That was what frightened him most – his right arm! His gun arm!

Then someone coughed.

'Be light in an hour.' It was a curt, raspy voice only a foot or so from him. His head turned painfully on a wrenched neck.

A man crouched in the entrance to the brush shelter. That was all he could tell – it was a man, pretty much shapeless under a torn slicker, blotched against the light of a small fire.

'Who're you?'

The blob grunted. 'It's usual to ask "Where am I?" But guess you know what you want to know. You can call me Cappy or Cap, whatever your inclination.'

The raspy, harsh voice somehow did not go with the choice of words. Here was a man who knew right well how to speak what was seen as 'proper' in the civilized world, but his voice was that of a roughneck from the cattle trails or the dark, dank claustrophobia of a miner's tunnel.

'Cap sounds all right for now, I guess.' There was a wary edge to the wounded man's voice, but if the other noticed he gave no sign. *Or did he? His eyes narrowed and there was more rigidity to the shoulders.* 'My horse?'

'Grazing with mine – strong animal that black gelding of yours. Good lines. Knew a deal about horses, once – what to look for, speed and endurance, ability in contrasting country, desert or mountain, unafraid of water. . . .'

Ringo's eyes were on the man's face now. 'Sounds

like a cavalry man talking.'

The hard, dark eyes lashed him like a whip and the mouth stretched into something slashed by a razor. But only for an instant. 'Or maybe a horse-thief. . . .' He let it hang.

Then he chuckled, wheezing a little, and it turned into a rumbling, wet cough. He spat over his shoulder so the saliva landed outside the brush shelter. *A man of hygiene!*

But the wounded man's throbbing brain couldn't hold such a thought for long and he passed out again.

Next time he was aware, the shelter was filled with watery sunlight, and the rain had stopped – even the drips were silent. He could see through the opening, glimpsed his rescuer crouching with his back to him over a small fire – maybe the same one as before. The smell of sowbelly and chilli beans made him salivate. He cleared his throat. 'I guess mebbe I could go some of that.'

A bearded face, grey and gaunt, stared at him with bleak, disconcerting gaze over a hunched shoulder. The slicker had been discarded to reveal a patched woollen shirt under a frayed vest, like that worn by railroad clerks.

'This chilli will make a dead man walk.'

The wounded man whispered, 'Mebbe I need the exercise.'

'Huh! Sense of humour, eh? Not a bad thing. Where I come from it was a necessity if you were to. . . .' He let the thought drift. 'Now it's my turn – who are you?'

A hesitation, long enough to make the man by the fire shift around and glare hard into the shelter. 'Well?'

'Call me Ringo.'

'That's all? Not Ringo "This" or Ringo "That"? Or perhaps "Something" Ringo?'

'Just – Ringo.'

'Hmm. The kind of name that covers a multitude of sins: can stand alone, or give ground to a Christian name, or retreat and make way for a surname – but Ringo it shall be, if that be your wish.'

'It is – Cap.' Ringo moved his lips slightly in a half-smile. 'Another – versatile name, I believe.'

Cap nodded slowly, turned back to his cooking. 'Thought you'd be feeling much more poorly than you're acting. That bullet just missed your lung, you know.'

'Missed? But I was spitting blood.'

'Don't doubt it. You have two broken teeth and they've cut the inside of your cheeks. A direct result of violence, I suspect.'

Ringo's tongue explored inside his mouth and he nodded as he located the lacerations. 'You speak like a doctor.'

'No, friend, but I have had some scant experience of helping a sawbones or two over the years.'

'I'm obliged for whatever you've done for me. In fact, I figured that river had done for me.'

The man called Cap was sober now. 'Friend Ringo, I enjoy a little humour but I have to tell you now that a little goes a long way with me.' He lifted a hand swiftly. 'It's just the way I am; I live a solitary life and

I have my own ways. If they seem to clash with yours, then you'll either have to accept them or, if that be asking too much, why – move right along.'

'You're a hard horse, all right, *amigo*. I can mostly take another man's ways. I wouldn't be ungrateful enough to question yours after you helping me.'

Cap said nothing, began dishing up two tin platters of food, came in crouching. With some heaving and a few grunts and involuntary complaints from Ringo, he sat the wounded man up against the brush wall, a worn grey blanket folded behind him. Ringo was sweating and pale by the time he was in position. 'I-I ain't too sure I can . . . eat right now after all.'

'Give it a few minutes. You'll settle down; it's the change in position. Your wound is healing well enough, just be careful not to break it open again.'

Something in the man's words made Ringo frown and ask, 'Again? How long've I been here?'

'Let me see.' Big, gnarled, calloused fingers with horny though reasonably clean nails, came up to the level of Ringo's eyes and a second set of fingers began to count off. 'Three days. This is the start of the fourth day since I pulled you from the river.'

'Hell! That's a surprise.'

'You were better not to know those last couple of day. There was a good deal of pain, I suspect, by the noise you were making – not that we could go anywhere.' He saw Ringo's puzzlement and added, 'Marooned. But the water level's slowy dropping. We'll be able to get to solid land by noon tomorrow, or the next day, or whenever, I'd guess. We could go now, with some little risk, but time is not all that

17

important to me any more. I've come to terms with it, you might say.'

'You might. But it's a strange remark.'

Ringo got no answer to that.

They ate, Ringo picking at first, then getting his appetite back. 'Man, that was good! You had some experience at cooking, too, Cap?'

The sober eyes held steady on him as he wiped his beard with a damp kerchief. 'I have had experience in many different things, my friend, not always willingly, but I have endeavoured to always make it a *learning* experience. A man never knows when a little half-forgotten knowledge will get him out of trouble.'

It was in Ringo to ask what kind of trouble, but he held back: to ask would require that he answer a similar question in return and he did not want to share confidences to that degree. *Not yet.*

'Wouldn't have any tobacco, I suppose?'

'Your assumption is correct. It's many years since I last smoked.' His face took on a sudden, musing look. 'Which is not to say that I don't approve of the weed, just got out of the habit – without much choice. In fact, it has served me well enough, even during my no-smoking time.' His hard eyes seemed to flicker. 'You're puzzled, but under certain circumstances, tobacco can be valuable, even act as a kind of currency.' The man suddenly seemed to realize he may have said more than he meant to and cut off abruptly. 'Or did you already know that?'

'Might've heard it somewhere,' Ringo said quietly, eyes steady on that gaunt face, screened by the beard

18

– hairy enough to even be thought a disguise, if he were uncharitable enough to dredge up such a thought. 'Happens amongst soldiers, the smokers and non-smokers. Jail, too, I believe.'

The bearded one's expression did not change and his voice was steady.

'I have your guns drying in the sun. But I am not very familiar with this latest model cartridge-shooting single-action Colt. I will leave it to you to disassemble and service. The same with your repeating rifle. I can shoot one well enough but have not yet taken one apart to study the workings. If it were a Trapdoor Springfield or Sharps—' He stopped again, abruptly. 'Tell me when you feel up to doing something about your firearms. Perhaps you can even show me their intricacies.'

Ringo met and held his gaze and took a few seconds before he nodded. 'I can do that – right now, if that's OK.'

'My friend, *you* are the only one who can tell if it is "OK".' The man who called himself Cap or Cappy heaved to his feet, smiling thinly. 'I'll get 'em for you.' He paused at the entrance, looking back. 'I somehow saw you as a man who would not wish to be without working firearms any longer than necessary.'

He ducked outside and Ringo frowned at the low, empty opening, saying softly, 'Uh-huh. And I think I have you picked, too, *mi capitan*. You're army, but a long time back, before the Colt Peacemaker single-action became the most wanted side-arm in the coun-try. And before Winchester and Henry repeaters could be bought at any general store, and the old army-issue single shots were curiosity pieces, or the weapon of choice of only a few diehards.'

Then, Ringo, twisting awkwardly, adjusted the blanket Cap had placed behind him, not without some wrenching pain. While he was catching his breath he saw some faded printing along one edge. He was just able to read the words:

Territorial Prison – Canyon City – Colorado.

CHAPTER 2

RIVER RAID

The river beat them. Ringo blamed himself because he wasn't up to making the crossing of the wide expanse of muddy water to the mainland. It was still flowing fast, would need a good deal of manoeuvring of the mounts and the pack mule Cap had brought out of the brush. This latter animal was loaded with gear, covered by a tarp. Ringo was curious, but never asked what was carried on the old weathered *alforjas* pack-frame. But he guessed digging tools by the shape of the bulges, perhaps a prospector's tin dish – Cap seemed at pains not to mention it or draw attention to it in any way.

'I'll be OK now,' Ringo told him after the second unsuccessful attempt to cross the river, feeling far from OK. 'You go ahead, I'll follow, mebbe tomorrow or next day.'

Coughing, the older man swivelled around in the saddle. 'Your version of "OK" and mine seem to differ – I damn near had to rescue you all over again just now.'

They were both wet from their attempts to cross the turbulent waters. Ringo, breathless, stiff, covering the surges of pain he was experiencing, waved a hand. 'What I mean is, I'll be able to manage alone in another day or so. You got places to go, no need for you to hang around waiting for me.'

Cap smothered another cough, folded his hands on his saddlehorn. 'You like to make people's minds up for 'em, eh?'

Ringo frowned. 'That's not it – just don't want to hold you up in whatever business you're about.'

The bearded man sighed. 'You seem set on splitting up. Time don't matter so much to me, now. Told you once – you ought to listen.'

Ringo stiffened a little. 'I listen. Cap, you do what you like. I feel I need to spend another day or so here. I'll be happy enough to have your company, but if you *should* decide there's some pressing need to cross now. . . .'

Talking, growing impatient and on the verge of anger, Ringo absently dropped his hand to the butt of his holstered sixgun. He saw Cap stiffen, gaze sharpening. The man looked from the hand to Ringo's face. 'I don't aim to give you any kinda argument that'd call for gunplay, Ringo.'

The younger man, somewhat embarrassed, let his hand slide back to his thigh. He nodded jerkily. 'Habit.'

'I kind of figured it was instinctive. But no matter. I'll stay on and see you right. If we need to, we can come to the parting of the ways whenever we cross. There's a town to the south, Riverton – you'd've passed through it, most likely. We can share a farewell drink there.'

Ringo stared soberly. 'Not in that town.'

Cap was silent and motionless for some seconds, then nodded gently. 'Then we'll put that notion on the shelf for now. Sometime we might meet up again.'

'Possible. So, you crossing now?'

Cap shook his head. 'I'll wait for you. Start a job, I like to see it through – habit.'

Half-smiling, Ringo said, 'Well, let's go build a fire. One reason I'm reluctant to leave you: I'll miss your sowbelly and chilli beans.'

They wheeled their mounts and rode the few yards back into the brush to their original campsite.

During the night, they found out it would have been better to leave that morning as originally planned. Cap's cough started up so both were half-awake when four men hit the camp with all guns blazing, just before moonrise.

They came in on foot and that was likely what saved Ringo and the bearded man. It also meant that the attackers knew the island better than Ringo and his friend, were able to cross safely to it from another direction. Their horses must be tethered at the far end – it was a surprisingly large island for this part of the river, which was more than a mile across here, even wider while the flood waters swirled.

But those thoughts shot through his mind with the speed of light as he rolled out of his blankets, feeling the twinge in the still-healing wound under his shoulder. Bullets thudded into the ground, scattered twigs, dead leaves and the dying fire. He heard Cap give a hard curse.

'You hit?' Ringo dived headlong as he snapped the query, spotted the rising shadow of one of the gunmen and triggered the Colt whilst in mid-air. The man spun with a startled cry and the other guns momentarily fell silent – obviously they hadn't expected such quick reaction, or accuracy. Then, when Cap's sawn-off shotgun thundered, Ringo knew he was all right. The man favoured the riot gun although he wore a Colt as sidearm, had a Winchester in a saddle scabbard, both of which weapons Ringo had shown him how to maintain, clean and shoot. Someone yelled and suddenly the night was filled with muzzle flashes and throat-rasping gunsmoke, wild yells and a scream that told of another man mortally hit.

Cap's shotgun was silent and Ringo heard him swear as he fumbled to reload in the dark. He saw a figure rise up behind the bearded man, not two yards away: Cap's coughing had given away his location. Ringo snapped a shot, dropped hammer again, but it fell on an empty chamber. The man staggered and Cap, startled at the closeness of the killer, dropped his shells.

The attacker was only wounded and rose above Cap, bringing down his pistol. Ringo snatched up his rifle from the crumpled bedroll, dropping the Colt, and fired two shots at the menacing shadow quicker than a man could draw breath.

The raider spun and lunged away into the brush with a sob of pain, a hand to his head. Ringo's lead whistled about his ears. The remaining raider ran for the heavy shadow of the brush. Ringo fired, missed, heard boots thudding. He went after the killer, aware he was fighting for breath after only a few steps, his chest aching with each intake of air. He staggered, went down to one knee just as the fugitive turned, still running, and triggered.

Ringo rolled, rifle across his body, lever and trigger co-ordinating as he put a bullet through the man's chest. It hurled the raider into the dark and there was a sobbing, gurgling sound as he hit the ground.

Ringo sat down, lungs seared from the effort, head spinning, ears ringing. He coughed as gunsmoke swirled around him. He couldn't hear anyone moving, managed to get enough air to call, 'Cap. . . ?' No answer.

A few more steadying breaths and he used the smoking rifle as a lever to get to his feet. He swayed, the night shot through with lightning streaking behind his eyes. Twice he stumbled over bodies, one man barely alive, holding his belly, ripped open by Cap's shotgun it looked like. In the growing silver light as the moon lifted above ranges on the mainland, Ringo saw the pleading eyes staring right at him – there was no mistaking their message.

He hesitated, then lifted the rifle and put the killer out of his misery.

Cap was down, a shallow head-wound and another gouge just where his neck joined his shoulder, both bleeding. He was unconscious, but moaned and started to come round a little when Ringo washed the head wound with water. He put the canteen to Cap's lips and the man gulped, coughed, spraying water. He looked groggy, staring up into Ringo's face.

'We . . . OK . . . now. . . ?'

Ringo nodded. 'Three ready for burial. One got away.'

'Jesus! You are *good*, friend!'

'You ripped one up with that cut-down Greener.'

'But you accounted for the others! My God, wish I'd had half-a-dozen like you in my troop at Shiloh . . . but you likely weren't even born then. Twenty-five year ago.'

'I was around, only four or five years old, though. . . . I'm gonna have to cut some hair away, and try to get you outa your shirt – unless I cut that, too.'

He cleaned Cap's head wound and bandaged it, noticing an old scar amongst the dark hair, shot with a little grey. The man tentatively half-lifted his left arm. 'Can leave the neck – feels no more'n a scratch.'

Ringo said slowly, 'Not deep but bleeding plenty. Ruined your shirt where the bullet tore it up and all that blood and dirt. Best get it off so I can clean the wound.'

Cap seemed as if he would give him an argument and Ringo frowned. Then the bearded man said, 'What the hell! Do what you like.'

It was unnecessarily surly and Ringo pursed his lips, was going to leave things as they were but he knew that neck wound was in need of cleaning. Without any further hesitation he took his knife, pulled the loose shirt material away from Cap's back and cut it to the waist, spreading the two ends like limp, sodden wings, around the bony shoulders.

Then he reared back on his haunches. 'God almighty! What the hell happened here?'

The bearded man sighed. 'You like the pattern? The bastard who made those checks took pride in his work. Used to be a sailor on a limey ship of the line. They call him the Bosun. May the son of a bitch rot in hell.'

'I'd say that's where he comes from if he could do this to a man.' Ringo could not prevent himself from running his fingers lightly over the checkered pattern of raised scars and welts that covered Cap from neck to waist.

'There's a knack to it, you see: lay on the stripes with the right hand, then switch to the left side, criss-cross the thongs. Makes for a neat checkered pattern. The bastard had had a lot of practice. The warden and guards would bet on whether he would cut squares or diamonds in a man's back, and how long it would take. He has been known to lay on the right-hand stripes and have the doctor call 'Enough', cut the man down. Then he would leave him to sweat in his cell – alone – wondering when they'd come and get him for the rest of his punishment.'

He paused, seeing the attention Ringo was giving him, the horror of the picture conjured up reflected in the younger man's steel-grey eyes.

'Carried a lot of weight with our warden, did the Bosun. A man might be due another ten lashes, but that didn't mean Bosun would give them to him all at once. Oh, no. They could come in the middle of the night, drag you out, truss you to the whipping frame and he might lay on one or two and then you'd be taken back to the cell to wait . . . and wait . . . and wait, till Bosun was ready to lay on another two or three. Sometimes, a man would be trussed to the frame – encrusted with dried blood and bits of other men's flesh, it was rarely, if ever cleaned down – and simply left there. No lash. Totally alone. Just leave him hang from his bonds – expecting the whip every second, then maybe take him back to his cell – until next time. Hard on a man's nerves.'

'Surely someone killed the scum!'

'Scum's a good name for him – but, no, far as I know, he's still alive and no doubt getting his sadistic kicks from his cat-o'-nine tails. He keeps it in a little red flannel bag.'

'I've read about that little red bag and the "cat", with knots tied in the nine thongs. Part and parcel of life aboard those old British men-o'-war. But never heard of it used that way in a US jail . . . Colorado Territorial?'

There was a lifting query in his last words and he arched his eyebrows questioningly.

Cap stared back, face set in hard lines under the beard. 'There are some jails treat their prisoners worse than that, my friend – I've experienced several of them.'

Ringo frowned. 'I had you down as ex-army, not—'

'Not ex-jailbird?' cut in the other. 'Ringo, I'm an expert on jails. I've lived the last twenty-five years of my life behind bars and walls, transferred here and there – widening my experience, you might say.' Ringo was stunned and Cap frowned, studying him closely. 'You surely have a stronger stomach than that! Or, perhaps I underestimated your powers of imagination.'

Ringo cleared his throat, that steely gaze steady on the other's face. 'I'm not sure I *can* imagine spending that long behind bars – especially with treatment no decent man would show the worst kind of animal.'

Cap surprised him by shrugging, although he winced as the bullet-gouge oozed blood. 'Maybe I'll tell you about it some day.'

'I'll hold you to that.'

'You are . . . strange, friend Ringo. I feel an odd rapport with you. You know the word?'

'Means a kind of harmony, doesn't it? Not American, though.'

'French, I believe. They're good with those kind of words they tell me. Yes, harmony seems good enough. You don't feel it?'

Whatever Ringo felt towards this man he aimed to keep to himself. In fact, he felt kind of flummoxed. He smiled faintly: now that was a good word, appropriate. But he busied himself getting clean rags and some fresh water so he could tend to Cap's neck wound.

Neither slept that night, not deeply, anyway. They spread their bedrolls close together, loaded weapons

29

in hand or within easy reach, although Ringo told Cap several times he figured there would be no more danger now.

'Carnevan doesn't work that way.'

'He the one put the bullet in your back?'

'Uh-huh.'

'In Riverton.' Cap gestured vaguely to the south.

'Yeah – he's the sheriff there.'

The bearded man sat up with a jolt, immediately coughing and holding his bandage which showed signs of blood seeping through. 'He weren't among those dead men?'

He gestured vaguely to the brush and Ringo shook his head. 'No. Must've been the one who got away. Reckon I winged him, though.'

'So, you got law trouble.'

'Not exactly.'

'As the young maid said to her father when he asked if she was pregnant to the stable boy. Hell, Ringo, you got law trouble or not?'

'Well, Carnevan's the law in Riverton all right, but no one ever swore him in legally and pinned a star on him. He did it himself, took over, had mebbe a half-dozen or so hardcases to back him up.'

'But only four came here. You sure you never met no more in Riverton?' When Ringo merely shrugged, Cap whistled softly, added, 'I'm kind of glad I made friends with you.'

Ringo smiled faintly. 'I'm a friendly feller, most times – long as no one pushes me around.'

'And Carnevan did some pushing?'

'Figured he had cause.'

The bearded man nodded gently and didn't ask any more questions. 'Looks like we both wait before moving on.'

There could be more meaning in those words than the obvious, Ringo thought. But they left it at that and fell silent till the sun came up and then rebuilt the fire, dragged the dead men into the brush and caught their spooked mounts, unsaddling, before turning them loose.

Cap hadn't lost his touch with the skillet and sowbelly, although he looked pale and gaunt and complained of a headache that was worthy of a kick from a stallion.

'Damn arm's stiff, too. Won't be mixing no corn pone or batter for a spell. Or pullin' on cinch-straps.'

After a moment, Ringo said, 'Maybe I can do the awkward things for you. I can cook a little – ain't poisoned myself yet.'

Cap looked up sharply, wincing again at the twinge in his neck. He studied Ringo, nodded slowly. 'You've a hankering for us to travel together, huh?'

'For a spell, leastways.'

'You got business you'd rather do alone?'

'Some. I'll tell you when I'm ready to do it.'

The bearded man was damn sure he would.

But what was it about this Ringo? Cap wondered. The bearded man was a loner himself, *liked* being alone, was even able to stay isolated in the crowded prisons, and quite content that way.

Normally, he would have ridden out long ago. But here he was, not only beholden to this young drifter, but even happy enough with his company.

31

Must be the way he handles his guns, Cap decided. Yeah, that was it – keep him around until he settled a few scores, make use of his gun prowess, then ride on.

If he was able. . . .

CHAPTER 3

HOLLOW VICTORY

'You knew Carnevan well before.'

It was a statement, not a question and, riding over the crest of a ridge, keeping to what timber there was, Ringo barely glanced at Cap as the man put his shaggy dun alongside him, making his remark.

'We tangled once or twice.'

'Scores to settle?'

'He thinks so.'

The words had a finality about them that prevented the bearded man from asking for more details. He could tell the subject was a touchy thing with his young sidekick. But, if they were to ride together, even for a short time, some more cards had to be laid on the table by both of them.

'Reckon you noticed that old scar across my scalp when you were treating this one.' He touched his bandage.

Ringo nodded but didn't speak.

'Almost older'n you – got it in a duel.'

That brought Ringo up straight in the saddle. 'Would've been a long time back.'

'Man I fought made insulting remarks about my wife, in her absence, at a Confederacy fund-raising. It was only gossip he was passing on: don't think he even knew it was my wife he was talking about when you get right down to it.'

'Wouldn't matter.'

Cap looked sharply at Ringo, nodded gently. 'The way I felt. I was there: I'd heard him. So had a lot of others. Enough for me. I was in the army at the time.'

'A captain?'

Cap frowned at the interruption but nodded curtly. 'War had been running a year or thereabouts. The army frowned on duels, had a regulation prohibiting them, under pain of death by firing squad, but I arranged mine anyway.'

'Obviously you won.'

'Hollow victory, my friend: I was a long time recovering. I killed the other man, a civilian, important in munitions, supplying the South. His uncle was a general, Headquarters Staff – I see you're ahead of me.'

'Some. They found you guilty?'

'I had friends as well as enemies in the higher ranks, luckily. They got my death sentence reduced to jail time.' Cap's mouth tightened and he shook his head once, jerkily. 'Didn't do me any favours. If I'd been asked I wouldn't've thanked 'em – not when the court martial handed me down a twenty-year term.'

'Be mighty daunting, I reckon.'

'More'n that. I'd figured when the war finally ended in a couple of years I'd be turned loose. But by that time most of my friends were dead and my enemies outnumbered the ones I had left. My papers were marked "No Remissions".'

'You said you'd been in jails for the last twenty-*five* years.'

Cap smiled grimly. 'Guess I was a bad boy. That checkered back was part result of it after a couple of escape attempts, the rest was an extra year here, another six months there – mounted up fast.'

Ringo was silent a spell, then asked, 'Your wife?'

Cap's face didn't alter, but Ringo had the notion that this was something the man had worked at – keeping a closed, unreadable look when asked that question. 'Died.'

Ringo didn't push it.

'Guess you still have some scores to settle.'

'Slowly getting round to 'em.' Cap gave him a straight look, coughing suddenly. 'Damn jails didn't help my health much. Lungs're shot: get a cold and I'm likely to end up with pneumonia. Which is why I dry off quickly and just about sleep in the camp-fire to stay warm as I can. You might've noticed my buffalo hide bedroll.'

Ringo had: a couple of times had wished for it himself when the cold rain was still falling.

'Belonged to one of the wardens – the one brought in the Bosun to keep the inmates in line.' He paused, seemed to debate whether to go on, then added, 'Retired before I left. Looked him up after I got out, though. He . . . donated the robe.'

He let it drift away. Ringo said nothing, nor showed anything, one way or another.

'I hope you'll be with me when I find the Bosun.'

Ringo gave him a steady look.'You know where?'

'Know where he might be.'

'We headed that way now?'

'We-ell, could make a slight detour to see your friend Carnevan – if you prefer.'

Cap straightened in the saddle, but Ringo wasn't looking at him, just riding along, generally studying the country they were passing through. 'Carnevan'll keep. Kind of looking forward to meeting this Bosun, though.'

'Good. Was wondering if I should hire you.'

'Who says you have to?'

After they reached the bottom of the rise on the far side of the mountain, Cap said, 'We're about square, you and me – doctoring each other's wounds and so on.'

'You keeping count?'

'No-ooo. But don't want you to feel beholden to me when I'm just as obliged to you for helping me out.'

'Then we're even-Steven. Anything from here on in will be out of friendship.' Ringo swivelled his sober gaze around. 'Suit you?'

'Sure – sure.' But, somehow, Cap didn't sound all that pleased with the idea. 'Been kind of short, though, our "friendship".'

'I've met men I've took to within seconds of shaking hands, others I've known for years and still wouldn't call 'em friends.'

'Aye, that's the way of it, all right, queer though it is.'

They fell silent, neither realizing they were both thinking the same thing right now: *they never had shaken hands.*

Ringo knew the man would use him just the same.

But he had no complaints.

Over supper – a spartan meal of canned beans and stale bread fried in bacon fat – Ringo said quietly, speaking for the first time in hours,

'What were you doing on that island, anyway?'

'You complaining?'

Ringo shook his head. 'Hell no.'

'I might's well ask what you were doing in the river.'

'Trying to reach the damn island. Figured Carnevan would send someone after me, even if only to see that the bullet he put in my back finished me off. I reckoned to hide out for a spell. Saw the island, tried to cross but underestimated the river, got caught halfway.' He swallowed some greasy bread, washed it down with a mouthful of coffee, watching Cap over the rim of the tin mug. 'Night birds are loud.'

'Huh? I don't hear any.'

'Must be there somewhere, 'cause I never heard you say what you were doing on that island in the first place.'

Cap stared then, smiled faintly. 'Pushing things a mite now, huh? OK. Guess you got a right. Told you

I fought a duel.' He jerked his head in the direction they had come. 'Took place on that island, only was just a butt-naked sandbar those days. Lot of vegetation's grown up in twenty-five years.'

Ringo chewed and drank more coffee. 'Can't believe it was just nostalgia brought you back.'

'No. My second was a lieutenant from my regiment: good soldier, good friend. The civilian offered him five hundred dollars in gold not to load my pistol – just powder, no bullet.'

'Man must've been scared white.'

'Yeah. Was the booze courage talking at the fund-raising, I knew that. But the words had been spoken and a lot of people heard them. I was set on going through with the duel no matter what – my lieutenant knew that. But he accepted the five hundred in gold.'

'The hell you say!'

'And loaded my pistol just the same.'

He waited while Ringo thought about it. 'Told you the lieutenant was a good man. Too late to return the gold after the duel, of course, so he buried it. Just rode away from it.'

'Sure must've been loyal to you.'

'He was. But the civilian's friends caught up with him in Denver. He was found in an alley with a knife in his back. He'd left a sealed letter among his things for me and it eventually found its way to me in jail. All it said was, *You might find need of this when they finally turn you loose.* Like me, at that stage, he thought I'd be released when the war was over. There were directions where to find the gold, but like I said,

38

it was just bare hillocks of sand and a few rocks at the time of the duel and landmarks had changed on shore – I had me a helluva time working out where that gold could be. Could've been found by somone, or floods washed it away. But he was right: I had need of that money, so I camped there a spell, searching. I had time.'

Ringo stopped himself asking if the search for the gold had been successful. As it turned out, he need-n't have bothered. Cap made no secret of it.

'So, we come to a town we like, we'll get ourselves a bath and a haircut and shave, have a few drinks and a good meal and we'll both feel a helluva lot better. OK?'

'Sounds good, but – well, I'm a man likes to pay his way, Cap.'

'Me, too, and I admire you being the same, but this is something based on our friendship, remem-ber? I mean, you wouldn't want to insult me by refus-ing, would you?'

Their eyes met and held and after a moment, Ringo nodded slightly. They finished the meal and he asked quietly, 'Captain who. . . ?'

Cap snapped his head up, face thoughtful for what seemed like a long time. 'Tyrell. Ethan Tyrell. And you?'

The younger man's gaze never wavered. 'Just keep calling me Ringo.'

Tyrell's eyes narrowed, the jaw beneath the beard jutted slightly. Then he drew down a deep breath.

'OK. Cap's still good enough for me.'

'Then nothing's changed.'

'Except you know a lot more about me than I know about you.'

And Captain Ethan Tyrell didn't seem very happy about that.

No one knew Carnevan's real first name but he answered to Dutch readily enough.

Right now, he was using many different names, each one spat out with venom, mostly obscene, a goodly portion blasphemous.

His head was bandaged, bulging over his left ear, stained with blood and iodine. Reddened eyes turned up to the languid doctor just putting his bottles and a few minor instruments into his large black bag.

'How much of my goddamn ear did that bullet take?'

The medic moved his eyes, otherwise his body was still except for his hands closing the bag. 'I've already told you, Dutch – about the upper third. But, as I warned you, I may have to pare away a little more if proud flesh develops – I won't know for sure until the healing process is further advanced.'

Another spate of vituperation spilled into the gloomy room. It was nearing sundown and no one had yet lit the lamps. Dutch Carnevan eased back in his chair, his face still in the fading light coming through the dusty window, one floor up from the bustle of the street below but still collecting plenty of dust and insects and noise.

It was a face full of angles: heavy eye sockets threw shadows that deepened the effect of angularity. A rim of brow that held a single eyebrow – or gave that impression – stretched right across. The nose had a sharp bend in it, narrow and axe-bladed, the jawline hard-edged, and a thick frontier moustache softened the thin lips of the mouth. The whole was framed by tight-curled black hair. Despite that, he had no trouble attracting women, some of whom found his slightly brutal looks appealing. Now he took a coin from a front pocket of his vest and flipped it to the doctor who caught it easily.

'Don't you neglect me, Doc! I gotta get on the trail of the son of a bitch who did this to me.'

Making for the door, Doc Belden threw over his shoulder, 'Send one of your men. You stay where I can make sure that wound doesn't become infected.' Hand on the now open door, he looked directly at Dutch. 'Or you could end up with no ear at all.'

If Carnevan could have reached the half-empty bottle of whiskey easily he would have thrown it. Instead, as the door closed, he heaved up in his chair and splashed some of the raw red liquid into a glass. He tossed it down, groaning aloud at unexpected pain in his ear that the jerky movement brought on. He sipped the second more cautiously, looking out the window now, across the roofs of the buildings on the far side of the street, hard, dark eyes pinching down as he let his mind wander back – way back to the man who was called Ringo. . . .

They had been pards, sidekicks, in those days, after they met in the stinking cells of a Mexican Border jail. Then some attacking *rebeldes* who had nothing to

41

do with them raided the miserable town and started tossing dynamite around. One stick blew down enough of the jail wall for them to walk free. *Walk? Run like hell more like it!*

Two startled rebels wheeled their mounts as the temporary prisoners staggered out of the dust. The Mexicans' surprise gave the *Americanos* a chance to haul them off their mounts, give each a kick in the head, grab a firearm of some kind and then get the hell out and across the muddy river – shallow at that section – with lead and Spanish curses buzzing around their ears.

Two of the Mexicans, inflamed by seeing the *gringos* taking their horses, came surging into the river. Dutch had a rifle but it was a bolt-action Mauser and he was not familiar with it. Ringo only had a pistol and he rammed it into his belt, snatched the rifle from Dutch and shot both Mexicans out of their saddles.

'Keep it!' Carnevan roared as they spurred away and Ringo made to hand him back the rifle. 'Gimme the sixgun!'

They were both familiar with this Border country, hid out in a small gulch with a clear view of frontal approaches for a couple of days. Hungry, Ringo shot a stray steer and when they were butchering it for steaks, saw the brand burned into the hide: a crude rendering of a broken horsehoe.

'Judas! Someone owns this!'

'Yeah, we do – now.' Ringo wiped the blade of his knife on some grass, rammed it into his sheath and began to wrap the meat in an old shirt that had been in the saddle-bags on the horse he had taken from the Mexican rebel.

'Let's get the hell outa here,' Dutch said nervously. 'Don't you know that brand? Belongs to Kelso Bannerman.'

Ringo paused in his movements, then nodded and continued wrapping, but much faster now. 'Right! Let's go!'

They nearly made it, but a bunch of riders came out of the chaparral and surrounded them, all with drawn guns.

'You see that tall tree yonder, you rustlin' bastards?' snapped the man who was the obvious leader, middle-aged, face seamed with years of outdoor Border living. He spat. 'You gonna get a damn good view from there – when we hoist you up at the end of a rope.'

The others – five of them – laughed and someone said 'Hope they knows how to dance, Musty!'

'Yeah,' added another, grinning tightly. 'The good old Rio Two-step!'

Dutch and Ringo had their hands in the air now, both dry-mouthed. Then Dutch leaned forward a little and one of the men swiped at him with his gun barrel, knocking his hat off, making the man sway in the saddle. But the blow hadn't connected properly or Dutch would have been sprawled on the ground. He snatched at the horn, pulled himself upright and edged away from the belligerent rider. He looked at Musty, the man starting to tie a noose in his lariat.

'Musty? That wouldn't be Mustang, would it? Like in Mustang Kilby?'

The tough-looking small man paused with the hangman's noose only partly fashioned, squinted. 'You'd be?'

'Dutch Carnevan. Your brother knew me.'

The clearing was silent now, all eyes on Musty. 'By hell! You're the one brung him outa the desert with that bullet in his chest, carried him across your shoulders?'

Dutch managed to look suitably humble as he nodded. 'He was my pard,' he said simply.

There was murmuring amongst the Broken Horseshoe riders now, all watching Mustang Kilby – it was his decision. The man chose to delay it by turning to Ringo. 'Who's this?'

Dutch hesitated. 'Calls himself Ringo. We kinda met up in a Mex cesspool they calls a jail at Teconda Wells.'

Musty seemed suspicious. 'Never heard of no one ever leavin' that place, 'less it was feet first.'

Dutch hurriedly told him about the rebels raiding the town.

'Why were you there in the first place?' asked one of the riders, earning himself a hard glare from Kilby.

Carnevan scratched at his left ear. 'We-ell, there was this *señorita* – I knew she was married, but not who to. Turned out to be the local *jefe*.'

The men liked that, imaginations swirling. Musty's face didn't change as he swivelled his eyes to Ringo. 'You?'

'Believe it or not, I was just about to – borrow – Dutch's horse when the *jefe* sent his *guardia* for him. They scooped me up in the net, figured I was with him.'

The riders liked that, too, and guffawed, traded a few rough remarks with Ringo who smiled gently.

'We've been on the run two days,' Dutch said suddenly. 'Nigh on three. Nothin' to eat, nothin' the two days before that we spent in the hoosegow, neither. We was *hungry*, Mustang!'

'Never noticed any brand on that steer till we was butchering it,' added Ringo, Mustang's eyes swivelling towards him. The man grunted, stared, then began to recoil the lariat and Ringo breathed again.

'Dutch, you tried to save my brother's life. I'm obliged for that. He died, but he went peaceful under laudanum the sawbones gave him. I work for Mr Bannerman and I'm obliged to do my duty by him, too. But I ain't gonna lynch you now.' The men stirred uneasily and Kilby added quickly, 'I'm gonna take you back to the ranch and let Mr Bannerman decide.'

It was a reprieve, but when they reached the spread, they were locked in an underground root cellar and were told Bannerman wouldn't be back from El Paso for another two days.

They were treated reasonably and after a meagre noon meal, Ringo asked quietly, 'You really carry his brother out of the desert across your shoulders to a sawbones?' Carnevan nodded a little absently. 'You must've been feeling kindly.'

Dutch snapped his head around, then a slow smile began. 'I needed the shade. Anyway, I was the one shot him in the first place.'

'Then why the hell did you drag him in?'

Dutch shrugged. 'Knew he was gonna die, but

45

figured it'd look good – me comin' outa the desert, trying to help a badly wounded man. Hell, they treated me like a hero for a while. When they told me his brother was on the way in – I slipped away durin' the night.'

'Just like a true, humble hero, huh?'

Dutch nodded. 'Now, with a little luck, it might pay off,' adding under his breath, '*For me, anyways. . . .*'

No one else counted.

CHAPTER 4

POTHOOK

They lost a day when Cap Tyrell's head wound suddenly gave him trouble: shattering headaches, disturbed vision, nausea and vomiting. He fell out of the saddle and after getting him into the shade and placing a wet cloth over his forehead, Ringo sat back on his hams, studying the older man.

'That jail time's sapped my strength more'n I figured. Know I've got concussion. Seen enough of it during the war and they put me in the prison hospital to help out a few times.' Tyrell managed a weak smile. ' 'Course that was before that sadistic warden came. When *he* put me in the hospital, it was as a patient. Courtesy the Bosun.'

Ringo nodded, wishing he had a cigarette. 'I've seen concussion. You run across it often, trail-herding. Got no medicine so all you can do is rest up – and I mean rest.'

Cap Tyrell felt too poorly to argue and nodded

gently. Then Ringo spotted some willows fringing a nearby waterhole, scraped some bark into a tin mug and boiled it in water over a small fire.

Tyrell was drifting in and out of consciousness and there was some trouble getting him to drink the mixture but Ringo managed to get a good portion of it down his throat. It set him coughing for a bit and he glared up with reddened eyes. 'It'll help your headache,' Ringo assured him.

Cap didn't answer and although he had a restless night, moaning and, once, calling out, come next morning he was considerably better. More willow-bark mixture, a little coffee, and some hardtack and Cap rested. By mid-afternoon, Ringo had had enough of Tyrell's bellyaching about lying around and said, 'To hell with it! Just quit griping! But you fall outa the saddle again, I'm gonna leave you lie where you land.'

Tyrell worked up a smile. 'It's a . . . deal.'

But he managed all right, swayed a little but was fast regaining his strength. They camped that night just over the crest of a ridge and saw some lights below, at least five miles away.

'That ought to be a tank town called Pothook,' Ringo said. 'Trains top up with water there on their way to the beef markets.'

'I've heard of it: some of the other convicts spoke of it, but they made it sound like a kind of badman's hang-out.'

'Used to be. Likely still pretty tough, but they're a mite more civilized since they built the railroad and the water tanks.'

'Well, say we check it out in the morning, OK?' Cap yawned long and luxuriously, shaking his head gently. 'I'm plumb tuckered.'

Ringo gave him no argument and, taking normal precautions to hobble the mounts and shield their camp-fire, they turned in.

The two huge water tanks stood on stilts, looking like tall buildings through the heat-haze. They approached Pothook in the mid-morning sunshine which glinted off the hairpin bend of the river that gave the town its name. There were large cattle pens built off to one side of the tanks, with several raised loading chutes fronting on to the polished silver of the railroad tracks.

'Damme, it's a full-size railhead for cattle!' breathed Tyrell.

'Looks that way,' Ringo agreed and nodded to the scattered buildings a half-mile or so away from the siding. 'Last time I was here, there were no more'n half-a-dozen houses. Shacks mostly.'

'More like a hundred now.' Tyrell suddenly grinned and stroked his dust-clogged beard. 'You see smoke coming from me, it's them Confederate dollars burning a hole in my pocket!'

The town sure had grown since Ringo had last seen it. At that time, it was a dump, not even marked on the map as the railroad slowly edged out on to the plains, crossing the river by a high log-trestle bridge, and running in a long glide downslope to the tight bend where they decided to site the water tanks for future freight trains.

The underground wells they chose were also used

by hard men heading for the hills beyond and none of them liked the idea of the railroad spreading out this far: it would bring civilization in some form and they were not men who cared much for people and their homes and farms. The railroad camp was full of roughneck gandy-dancers and muscle-bound labourers from all over the world then. Even a few Chinese.

Ringo had been travelling with Carnevan: they had just had a lucky escape from lynching down at Bannerman's Broken Horseshoe. The hard old rancher had listened to Mustang Kilby tell him about Dutch bringing in his wounded brother from the desert, grunted and looked at Ringo.

'And who you got to speak for you?'

'Myself.'

That brought a guffaw from the crew and even Kelso Bannerman himself gave a faint smile.

'Well, won't ask you. I've a notion you'd paint a pretty damn good picture for me.'

Before Ringo could answer, Carnevan said, 'Reckon I can vouch for him, Mr Bannerman. He's a good man, with gun, rope and hosses. We both are, and was wonderin' about jobs, ridin' for Broken Horseshoe—'

'Well, quit wonderin' because I ain't offerin' any. You can have a grubsack of vittles. Be clear of my land by sundown, or Mustang's rope's gonna get stretched after all.'

That was it and Ringo felt relieved and even grateful. But Dutch Carnevan wasn't a man to count his blessings and be satisfied.

'Noticed some cows grazing way back at the far

end of a gulch before Mustang caught us,' he said, as they rode clear of Bannerman's. 'Didn't see any guards.'

'So?' Ringo asked warily.

'Hear there's a railroad camp east of here – they could always use a coupla steers. They get beef-hungry workin' for that old Spaniard.'

'What old Spaniard?'

'*Manual Labor*!' Dutch laughed, reached out and slapped Ringo on the shoulder. 'Hell, fancy you fallin' for that old one!'

Ringo smiled good-naturedly. 'Met him myself a few times. You ain't thinking of wide-looping some Broken Horseshoe steers?'

'We can use the dough. The railroaders'll pay top money – and then some.' He saw Ringo's hardening face and added quickly, 'Hell, Bannerman didn't have to kick us off like a couple of saddle tramps!'

'That's what we are, Dutch.'

'Well, I don't aim to be one with empty pockets.' He lifted the reins. 'You comin'? Or I got to do this myself?'

'Ain't the right thing, Dutch. Bannerman coulda hung us and been within his rights.'

'Aaah – what rights? Them the big-time cowmen have made for 'emselves? Take a good look and you'll see the so-called rights are only right for them! All one-sided.'

Ringo had to admit that, but that's the way things were. The war was over and the West had changed, was still changing. Men like them had no choice but to move with the times.

'You're behind the goddamn times if you believe that, Ringo! It's first in, best served these days. I been behind the door long enough. I'm moving out where the action is, going places – my way. Tag along if you want – if not, then *adios*!' Dutch touched a pair of fingers to his hatbrim in a mocking salute. 'Been nice knowin' you.'

He started to wheel his mount, but hesitated, obviously wanting Ringo to join him, then swore softly when the man made no such move. Dutch swung his mount away and spurred across the edge of the plain, disappearing into the brush. Heading directly for where he said he had seen those grazing cattle. . . .

Ringo was never quite sure afterward, why he impulsively spurred after Dutch, calling his name.

'You going to sleep in the saddle?'

Ringo jerked his head up, startled by Cap Tyrell's sharp query, bringing him back from his reverie. He saw they were approaching the first of the high water tanks now and followed Cap into the shade under the stand. Thick trees had been used for supports. The horses drank where water had pooled, seeping endlessly from heat-expanded seams in the tanks on the high platforms. The men drank from their canteens, aiming to refill them before heading up towards the town. There was no sign of life down here by the tracks.

'When was you here last?' Cap asked.

'Maybe five years back.'

Tyrell squinted, canteen halfway to his mouth. 'That don't have a happy ring to it.'

Ringo smiled, shaking his head. 'I've fonder memories of other towns.'

'You by yourself when you was here?' Cap asked shrewdly and Ringo sighed, shaking his head.

'Dutch Carnevan was with me.'

'Uh-huh.' Cap waited expectantly and after a while Ringo thumbed back his hat and said, 'We sold some beef to the railroad gangs.'

'Good profit?'

'Pretty good – seeing as the cows never cost us anything in the first place.'

Their gazes met and Cap moved a little unsteadily towards a low crossbeam, sat on it. 'Tell me about them cows while I rest up a mite and get my wits about me.'

'The day you don't have your wits about you, I'll know you're dead.'

Cap chuckled and Ringo leaned his slim hips on the crossbeam and scratched his nose.

'I knew it was a mistake when I went along with Dutch's idea to cut out a few cows from Bannerman's herd. . . .'

Tyrell whistled softly at mention of the rancher's name but said nothing, looking attentive.

This far down the trail, Ringo couldn't quite remember how he had rationalized things to himself so that he went along with Dutch Carnevan's plan. But they widelooped four steers from the grazing herd after dark and managed to get away without disturbing any of the Broken Horseshoe cowhands who were supposed to be guarding them.

They lost one animal in a crumbling arroyo, had to put it out of the misery of two broken legs, the loss of an eye and some bad gashes. They didn't dare use a gun so Ringo cut its throat. Carnevan was more interested in riding on and catching up with the other three steers that were still running. The railroad gang bought them readily enough but Dutch complained, 'Damn Mick foreman! Knows they ain't our steers or he wouldn't've haggled so much.'

'It's a good enough price – be glad of it.'

'This's gotta be split down the middle yet!'

'You can have my share.'

Dutch snapped his head up, frowned, studying Ringo's sombre face. 'By hell, you mean it, don't you? You got one of them pesky things they calls a conscience, ain't you? Now its give you a bellyful of flutters and you're showin' yaller!'

Ringo tensed. 'You're forking the wrong bronc, Dutch. OK, I have a conscience, but I like to think of it as a kind of code for a man to act by.'

'Oh, Jesus!' He crooked an arm and ran the other over an imaginary fiddle with an imaginary bow, humming a few mournful notes. 'Want a kerchief to dab your eyes?'

Ringo could see trouble looming and didn't want it: he wasn't a man who would step aside when trouble came at him, but if he could walk around it, that's the move he preferred to make.

He turned to his horse. 'See you around, Dutch.'

He was half mounted when Carnevan came at him. The man jumped and grabbed Ringo's belt at the rear, heaved back, using his body weight to throw the unprepared man several feet. By the time Ringo hit the ground sprawling, the breath gusting out of him, Dutch Carnevan was crouched on all fours and came in like a bull buffalo, with head lowered.

A little dazed, Ringo was just starting up when Dutch hit him, his head driving into Ringo's chest like a battering ram, knocking him down again. Carnevan reared up and swung a boot into Ringo's side. The man grunted, clapped a hand against his throbbing ribs, twisted his head aside from a second kick, deliberately waited for the third – and grabbed Carnevan's boot in both hands. He twisted, baring his teeth with effort. To avoid having his ankle badly twisted or even broken, Dutch had to go with it. He yelled an obscenity as he was spun like a top and ended up on his back. Blazing eyes raking Ringo's hard face, Dutch used hands and feet as he crab-crawled away on his back. Then he rolled over to hands and knees, thrust up and ran a few feet before suddenly stopping and turning sharply.

Ringo, already moving in, knew that old trick and halted just out of Dutch's reach, fists cocked. Dutch made his lunge automatically before he could hold back – and threw himself well into range of Ringo's fists. The hard knuckles drove again and again into Dutch's startled face, changing its appearance as blood squirted from the squashed nose, the split lips, a tooth showing through a rubbery lower lip, the left eye starting to close, the right one already half-blinded by blood oozing from the split skin above the brow.

Dutch Carnevan had always prided himself on his

fighting: he could take punishment as well as dish it out. But this time he was taking it all. They were solid, driving blows – and Ringo hadn't finished with him yet.

His fists hammered down across Dutch's chest, sank into the arch below his ribs, causing Carnevan to double up, face corpse-like with the violent snatching of his breath and the impact on his very heart. His legs buckled and Ringo moved back a step to give himself room to swing.

His fist cracked against Dutch's jaw with a sound like a plank falling. Carnevan spun and twisted away across the slope, sprawling limply, arms loose like a rag doll's. He slithered down, gravel and dirt adhering to the sticky blood on his flesh, rolled to a stop in a contorted heap.

The gangers from the railroad had come up from the railbed they were building when they had seen the fight start. These rough men looked at each other and then gave their attention to Ringo who was dabbing at a cut ear with a grimy kerchief. The foreman, a long-upper-lipped Irishman in soiled flannel undershirt and mud-spattered whipcord trousers, pushed stringy hair up from his craggy face.

'An' just what in the name of Old Nick was all that about, brother? We thought you two were pardners.'

Chest heaving, Ringo held the kerchief over the bleeding ear and said, 'Likely won't matter to you, but – the cows we sold you were wide-looped.'

'Ye're meanin' rustled.' The Irishman spat, nodding. 'Aye, well we knoo that. Ranchers hereabouts don't sell us their beef: they reckon the railroad's takin' their graze away. Ain't got enough between the ears to see what it's gonna mean when this same railroad opens up the beef market through here.'

Ringo nodded. 'So long as you know.'

The man squinted, curious. 'You'd be an odd man out, so you would, brother – you an' a conscience.'

Ringo shrugged, walking towards his patient horse now. Dutch Carnevan was still sprawled bloody and unconscious. 'Guess it was the way I was brought up.'

The man looked wistful for a few moments. 'Aye. Lot to be said for family – an' a fayther who likes to give his son-an'-heir the right outlook on life. First-born, are you?'

Swinging into saddle and settling with a grunt of pain or stiffness, Ringo looked down at him. 'Thing is, the man who brought me up wasn't my father.'

'Well now, kin or a friend of the family would know what kind of upbringin' was favoured. The Good Lord'll bless him for it.'

Ringo hesitated. 'Wasn't quite that way. But after seeing how some men out here behave, *I* bless him for taking the time to give me some principles to live by.'

The Irishman reached up abruptly with a big gnarled hand, the nails broken and clogged, like all the creases in the leathery flesh, with dirt and dust.

'An' I'm thinkin' they found a ready home. I'll be proud to shake your hand, brother – you got a name?'

The hands gripped. 'Call me Ringo.'

'Aye. 'Tis a name I'll remember. I'm Paddy – sometimes Spud. Like 'most every son o' the Green who's come to this grand land.'

Ringo grinned. 'Don't overdo it, Paddy. I've a little Irish blood in my own veins they tell me.'

'Then may the spirit of St Patrick ride with you.'

Ringo lifted the reins but still hesitated as he saw Carnevan starting to stir. 'What'll you do to him?'

'Aw, well, we got our beef which we been cravin' and the price was not too unreasonable. We'll dab a little iodine on him here an' there, and mebbe give him a swig of genuine Blarney Dew before sendin' him on his way.'

Ringo nodded. 'I don't want to have to kill him, so tell him I went south.'

He rode out – to the west.

Captain Ethan Tyrell hitched a bony butt-bone into a more comfortable position on the tank support and ran a tongue around the inside of his lower lip.

'Was that your fallin'-out? I mean, it don't seem all that bad, an' if the gangers treated Carnevan the way they said they would, he shouldn't have too many complaints.'

'Oh, I think the Irishman kept his word, but Dutch had tangled quite a bit with the law. Later, after he moved on, he ran into a sheriff who had a wanted dodger on him, sworn to by some woman who'd accused him of rape. He'd told me about it one night when we were swapping lies over a camp-fire and the first cup of decent coffee we'd had in two weeks. It was laced with some redeye that'd somehow found its way into Dutch's saddle-bags and maybe that'd loosened his tongue some. Seems he never told but a few men about that woman, me being the last one. He got a couple years jail and all the time he blamed me for it.'

'Thinks you set the sheriff on to him.'

Ringo nodded, and waited. But Cap didn't ask the obvious because he knew it wasn't the kind of thing a man like Ringo would do.

'He must've been pleased to see you when you turned up in Riverton a little while back, and him wearing a badge.'

Ringo smiled crookedly. 'You could say that. Jailed me, arranged my 'escape' so he'd have a reason to come after me. I expect to see more of him.'

Quietly, Cap said, 'Will it come to guns, then?'

'Reckon so.'

'You don't seem worried.'

'Not as long as I can see him. What does worry me, though, is Dutch Carnevan doesn't mind shooting a man in the back.'

Cap frowned and lifted a hand, forefinger tapping the air. 'I've been puzzling over that name – Dutch Carnevan. I keep thinking about some kind of – massacre, every time you mention him.'

Ringo's face tightened a little. There was a space filled with silence and then, 'Dutch didn't come after me when I left these tanks after our fight. I was ready for him, lived on a knife-edge for a few days. Then I figured it'd be best if I laid my devils to rest, went out to meet him – like it or not, I knew it was killing time.' He paused briefly. 'It turned out to be a bad idea. . . .'

Ringo had set out, weapons oiled and primed, ready to end this thing, push it as hard as he had to, but get it finished one way or another.

It was dark when he reached the railroad camp and the Irish foreman told him Dutch had joined up with some of the hard boys from back in the hills. 'We heard he had a gunfight with the leader, killed him and took over.'

'He been raising hell?'

'Here and there – mostly "there", I'm happy to say. But there was a whisper certain ranchers are payin' him to hassle the railroad surveyors and they've had some aggravation – camps wrecked, wagons burned, instruments smashed.'

Ringo frowned. 'Why the hell would the ranchers want to keep the railroad out? It doesn't make sense.'

'Well, brother, it do in this way: when the railroad comes, this part of the Territory will be reclassified and there'll be a Government Ordnance Survey of the land.'

'Which'll mean a lot of so-called free range won't be able to be exploited by the ranchers like it is now,' cut in Ringo, nodding. 'Greedy sonuvers. No foresight.'

The Irishman spread his hands. 'Ain't that the way of things, brother?'

Ringo nodded: if any country knew about land-grabbing and greedy governments, it had to be Ireland.

When he left, instead of riding west again, he

paused, turned north, towards the hills behind the tanks.

He hadn't found a place to camp for the night when he heard the rattle of gunfire to the east and south: in the direction of the surveyors' camp.

Rifle unsheathed, he set his mount in that direction. The gunfire was heavier now and he thought he heard Indian war whoops! It wasn't like even a bunch of renegade braves to attack at night when they could do a better job by waiting till dawn, just before the camp awoke.

But his panting horse stumbled at the edge of some trees and he swore as it gave a small whinny – luckily drowned by the war cries – and was favouring the left fetlock. Twisted a tendon or strained it! *There could be no chase now, dammit!* In any case, he was too late.

The camp had been set afire by hard-riding, half naked Indians. The bodies of the six-man survey party were scattered about and would be consumed by the flames. Ringo ducked as the war party grouped and started back, passing within ten yards of where he crouched, rubbing his mount's muzzle soothingly. He counted eight or maybe nine. The odds were too big, especially now his mount was lame.

Then he froze as an 'Indian' said clearly in Dutch Carnevan's voice, 'Well, boys, that was sure a good party. Be glad to get this goddamn dye off, though, so's we can go spend some of our hard-earned bucks on them whores they got stashed at the back of town.'

'Better scrub hard,' another voice said.' That big-titted Lila told me she won't take on no Injuns, or look-alikes, even if we are white underneath.'

'Lila might be surprised at what she finds *under-neath*,' Carnevan said and that brought laughter, quickly fading as the group rode on through the trees.

'*That's* what I heard in jail!' Tyrell said, as Ringo finished speaking. 'Army claimed it was an Injun raid, but later, a feller landed in our barracks and, bit of a swaggerer looking to get some prison respect right-off, reckoned he took part in that raid – under Dutch Carnevan. In there, you never know whether to believe that kind of thing or not but it seemed like gospel.'

'Well, that's what I saw.'

'And you never told the law?'

Ringo seemed uneasy at the question. 'Didn't seem much point – the surveyors were dead. There was no trace of the *Indians*. Aw, hell, Cap, I've lost a lot of sleep over it but I've never found the law all that friendly, so I just rode away from this neck of the woods.'

'Kept lookin' over your shoulder?'

'Wouldn't you?'

'Damn right! I'll be looking with you from now on.'

CHAPTER 5

LONG, LONELY TRAIL

The town called Pothook was no busier than most frontier settlements of the time when they rode up from the tanks, but the buildings were not so weather-worn and some paint looked reasonably fresh. Folk on the walks were dressed well enough and there was a good variety of items in the general store which, according to a large, tacked-on canvas sign above the street awning, was called 'Emerson's Emporium'.

'Seems like we might find us some decent clothes yonder,' opined Cap Tyrell, gesturing to the street front windows with their display of male and female mannikins dressed appropriately. 'But we'll have us a shave and haircut and bath first, OK?'

Ringo nodded and Cap said, 'Don't sound so enthusiastic.'

'I like to pay my own way, Cap. And I'm about bust.'

'Hell, you've earned whatever kind of high-time we have here.' He touched the head bandage. 'This counts plenty.'

'That only squares you for pulling me out of the river.'

'Hell almighty! Don't start! You and your damn independence.' Cap sighed. 'All right – look, I still need to know more about taking Colts and repeating rifles apart. You've showed me, but I'm way behind the times. I've got twenty five years to catch up, boy!'

Ringo seemed thoughtful before he replied, 'Well, have to admit I did think you were slower in picking things up than I expected.'

Cap hesitated. 'They put me inside second year of the war, Ringo. The South was mostly fighting with whatever guns folk had had on their farms or ranches. Flintlocks and muzzle-loaders. Long as it went *bang* at the right time was all they worried about. They were the only guns I knew.'

'OK! I don't mind showing you *again!*' He smiled thinly. 'Even again, *and again.*' But he couldn't help wondering how come an officer even that early in the war hadn't had at least some experience with the more technical advances in firearms that were just appearing.

Ringo hardly recognized Tyrell after their visit to the bath house and the barber's – *Muff Ingram's Tonsorial Parlour* to give it the name that was written in gold-leaf across the street window, traditional red-and-white striped poles each side of the door.

64

Tyrell's face looked strange, pale and fishbelly-white where his beard had been. His eyebrows had been trimmed and the barber had even put a fresh bandage on his head.

'If I gotta cover up that fine haircut I just give you, at least it's gonna be with a clean bandage.'

Cap waited until Ringo had had a hair trim and a shave and looked better for it, younger than Cap expected, but that iron jaw and the wary, hard-set eyes hadn't changed.

'Ladies are gonna be queuing up to get you in their parlour,' Tyrell allowed, taking a gold fifty-dollar coin from a leather poke attached by a thong to his trouser belt and hanging down inside his new trousers.

The barber examined the coin, lips pursed. There was only one other customer waiting now and he was easing himself into the chair, ignoring the group near the front of the shop. The barber held up the coin briefly to the street window. 'I can't change this, man, not for a two-bit haircut.'

'Got nothing else.' Cap arched his eyebrows quizzically at Ringo who shook his head. 'Gave what change I had to the bath-house woman.'

The barber's yellowed teeth tugged briefly at his lower lip. 'Look, reckon I can trust you fellers not to quit town without payin'. Go over to the bank an' ask for Pres Arnold. He's the manager and he collects coins.' Handing the gold piece back to Cap, he added in a lower tone, 'That's an unusual coin, mister – Confederate Mint mark. Pres could offer more'n the fifty it's got stamped on the face. Watch him, though, you might have to give him a nudge or two.'

Pres Arnold, after some deliberation and checking up on coin values in a well-thumbed book he took from his desk drawer, said, 'Mind if I ask where you got this?'

Cap tensed a little and Ringo wondered if the middle-aged, sleek bank manager noticed. 'It's genuine.'

'Oh, yes, I'm sure it's authentic. But these coins went out of production almost twenty-five years ago. I believe this is part of the last mint run and there-fore worthy of a premium – but I do like to know the provenance of any coins I'm considering buying.' He paused, seeing the blank faces of the others and smiled. 'Usually it's to do with previous owners but though I detect some signs of wear – scratches mostly – I will concede that this coin probably was never in circulation.'

'Been in the family for a long time,' lied Tryell eaisly. 'Turned up in an old cigar box belonged to my . . . brother. My elder brother.'

The bank manager nodded, seemed satisfied. 'Now – first, do you have any more?'

'Why?' Ringo asked. 'Does it make a difference?'

Pres Arnold studied Ringo's freshly shaven face closely, his smile returning – partially. 'Perhaps. I'm prepared to offer up to seventy-five dollars for this coin: that's quite a reasonable premium, I might add.'

'Sounds OK. You'd pay that for every coin like that?'

'Provided there wasn't a hoard of, say several hundred.' He added an explanation quickly. 'These coins are rare. To flood the market with hundreds – well, I'm sure you can see how their value would drop.'

Cap nodded. 'Sure. Keep 'em scarce and the price stays high.' Arnold merely stretched his smile. 'Happens I do have another – that'd be a hundred-fifty for the two?'

Arnold knew there was more, Ringo thought, but he was shrewd and Ringo saw the man wanted the coin, or as many as he could get for what he figured was a reasonable price.

'Well, yes, I think that's fair. I'll get your money – er – when I examine the second coin?'

Tyrell took a second gold piece from his poke and Arnold said casually, 'I'd keep these coins separate from everyday money that's in circulation – scratches can devalue them surprisingly quickly.'

Ringo placed a hand on Cap's arm as he made to pass the coin over. 'Seventy-five bucks'll see us through a wing-ding in this town, Cap. Whyn't you keep the other till we get to St Louis?' He watched the manager's face stiffen and change. 'There're bound to be coin dealers there who have more access to the market than Mr Arnold . . . Cap wants the best price he can get, banker.'

Arnold's mouth twitched under his thin moustache, looking from Tyrell to Ringo. 'If Mr Tyrell owns the coins, he should make any such decision.'

'Aw, I'll go along with my friend here,' Cap said, picking up on what Ringo was doing. 'Sounds like a good idea to me.'

Arnold went back behind his desk, picked up his magnifying glass and examined the coin he held. He raised his eyes without moving his head. 'All right. How many coins do you have? And what do you consider their value?'

'S'pose I said ten?'

Arnold's eyes widened. 'Ten! Well, that is a – manageable amount. They would not disrupt the market, if they were introduced – wisely.'

'You could get a hundred per cent profit with your expertise, I reckon,' Ringo said quietly, and Arnold's glare was cool. 'At least a hundred per cent.'

'You've done this kind of thing before!'

'Not exactly. But the folks who reared me had some genuine antique furniture; the woman I called Ma came from a well-to-do family in Scotland and had brought some mighty valuable pieces with her. I knew the local dealer wanted them and – haggling over price – he told me about introducing such things carefully into the available market.' He smiled ruefully. 'Nice, helpful feller – found out later he got more than twice what he paid me.'

Arnold suddenly laughed. 'A lesson well-learned, sir! All right, I will buy all ten coins from you for one thousand dollars.' His eyes took on an added sparkle, regarding Cap who was having trouble keeping a poker face. 'And, of course, you wouldn't want to risk carrying such a large amount of money on your person, so we could arrange for you to open an account with the bulk of it and draw on it as necessary . . . I'll pay you the balance in cash, of course.'

It was all accomplished in another twenty minutes and Tyrell and Ringo left the bank with burning holes in their pockets, the rest of the cash now in a bank account under Tyrell's name. Ringo reluctantly accepted his share – one hundred dollars – at Cap's insistence and they made for the biggest saloon, with a girlie section, a place called Paradise On The Prairie.

That night, at least, it lived up to its name for the pair of them.

When morning came, Ringo, red-eyed, holding his throbbing head, slurred, 'Gonna buy me some paint after – when I come alive. Can hardly see now.'

Cap squinted, looking more corpse-like than ever with livid patches of white on his ravaged face. 'What for, paint?'

'Gonna change that Paradise to Hell.'

Cap grunted. 'Give y' a hand – but later ─ much later. . . .' He groaned and rolled over where he lay.

Next time they came round they realized they were in the hay loft of the livery. The hostler's kid in his ragged-legged stained overalls stood with a pitchfork shaking in his bony hands staring at them with eyes like saucers.

'What you fellers doin' there?' Then seeing the obviously distressed men hawking and spitting and cursing their drumming heads, he called, 'Pa! Pa! We got us some visitors!'

The livery man was a tough-looking *hombre*, took the pitchfork from his boy and told him to go down below to the main stables and swill them out. He held the long-handled fork casually but the tines were

69

always pointing towards Ringo or Cap Tyrell.

'Seen you ride in. Got your broncs in my corrals out back and they gotta be paid for before you can have 'em.'

'Something's gotta be paid for,' said Ringo in a raspy voice, grimacing, spitting. 'Mouth tastes like the floor of one of your stalls!'

The man managed a lopsided grin. 'You went to Big Lila's, din' you? Yeah, thought so. Well, not that you have much choice, she runs the only cathouse in town – but my bet would be you two were so eager to have a good time, you let one of the gals, or mebbe one of the bouncers, see your roll.'

Ringo frowned at Cap who shrugged. 'Well, I – mebbe I did when I counted out some cash for the whore to go buy us some more whiskey.'

'Damn idiot!' Ringo growled, in no mood to mince words. He glared at the livery man. 'Would they've put something in that whiskey?'

The stable man lifted one hand. 'You never heard that from me – but I'd say you might have one almighty blast of a headache, a stomach that's doin' cartwheels and a taste you'd rather not try to describe in polite company. Right?'

Cap was coming back to normal now, jerked his head around and immediately regretted it. 'Oh, *Jesus*! You in it with 'em?' he demanded belligerently, but the livery man merely shook his head, not taking offence.

'You've a right to think that, I guess, but no – Lila keeps some rough company. They dumped you behind my corrals, in the weeds. One of my hounds found you and me an' my night hostler brung you up here – lots of snakes in them weeds.'

'We owe you our thanks, then,' Ringo said.

'You owe me more'n that – two dollars for corrallin' your mounts.'

'How about our beds?' gritted Cap a mite belligerently, gesturing to the hay.

'Aw, no one was usin' 'em, so no charge.'

They were both patting their pockets as they talked and Ringo said, displaying both trouser pockets turned inside out, 'You, too, Cap?'

Tyrell grunted. 'By hell, it's a damn long time since I was this foolish! 'Bout twenty years, I reckon!'

The livery man's eyebrows shot upwards but Ringo frowned slightly. *Twenty years? What happened to the other five Cap was supposed to have been in a jail?*

'Where're our guns?' Ringo asked.

'I got 'em downstairs – two Colt rigs and the Winchesters you had in your saddle scabbards.'

Ringo gave him a steady look. 'Mister, we owe you more than two dollars, all right. Can you think of anything that'll bring us halfway back to life?'

'Hot goat's milk with a shot of whiskey in it.'

Both men curled a lip. Cap growled, 'Hell, I'm almost throwin'-up again just at the thought! *Goat's* milk!'

'Speakin' from experience, friend. You gotta get a linin' back on that stomach, or you're gonna be lookin' for a quiet corner of Boot Hill to curl up in all day.'

They went along with him and remarked the potion tasted a lot better than they figured. 'I could taste chilli,' Cap added, kind of sickly and then both ran for the door, hands over their mouths.

When they returned their eyes were murderous. The livery man grinned. 'Now you'll feel better: got rid of the last of whatever Mickey Finn they slipped you. C'mon back to my rooms and I'll give you your guns – and a cup of coffee.'

They passed on the coffee, but took their guns eagerly enough. Both the hostler and Cap Tyrell watched Ringo check his Colt thoroughly and with expert speed. He said nothing as he strapped on his sixgun belt, then hefted the Winchester and checked that, too. 'You ready?'

Cap nodded and they shook hands with the livery man, who said his name was Gavin, whether first or last name he didn't say and they never asked. But as they left, he called, 'Mostly they'll be sleepin' now, but Lila keeps a couple rooms open out the back for daytime trade. There'll be some chuckers-out around . . . they carry hardwood billies.'

Ringo and Cap were grateful for the warning, but it didn't slow them down any: their still throbbing heads and anger at being gypped and rolled, drove them on.

Ringo, having the biggest boots according to Cap, kicked in the rear door and went in with rifle at the ready, Tyrell a step behind.

There were two women and three men, the latter trouserless and the former near naked. The men were obviously cowpokes in from the range, judging by the disarrayed clothing on the floor. Two of them dived for their guns under the pile but neither made it. Ringo stepped forward, dropped them both with swift, expert swings of the rifle butt and the third man backed up to the wall, hands high above his head. One of the whores screamed, but the older, ugly and more experienced one beside her slapped her face.

'Shut up, you stupid bitch!' She squinted at Ringo and Cap. 'Actin' like a couple soreheads won't do you no good, fellers. We got us protection here and if you care to look behind, you'll see just what I mean.'

'You look,' Ringo told Cap without taking his eyes off the ugly whore or the half-naked man against the wall.

'We got us company, Ringo, old friend. Two mighty sour-looking gents back here – with hard-wood billies and I think I see a knife handle in one's belt.'

'Well, take it off the son of a bitch and feed it to him,' Ringo said.

'Hey! I'm in my fifties!' And Cap started to cough so Ringo acted. He looked hard at the ugly whore who was crowing now help was at at hand. Ringo stepped forward, saying, 'I don't believe in hitting ladies – but reckon you don't qualify – and I recollect you from last night now, talking me into buying that spiked whiskey.'

On the last word his fist crashed into the whore's jaw and knocked her sprawling. She took the other one down with her. The cowboy figured to take advantage of the distraction and dived for the door.

'Let him go, Cap!'

Tyrell hesitated and the cowboy dived through – and immediately the closest bouncer, big and beefy and bald, swung his billy, cracking the man across the head. The cowboy dropped and by then Ringo was beside Cap. They both stepped outside. The second bouncer, a redhead with a harelip, sided his pard and they hefted their billies challengingly. 'Better think twice about this,' growled the redhead, the words slurred because of his disfigurement. Ringo remembered seeing him in the barber shop – with his ear hanging out when the barber told them to see the banker about their gold coin.

'*You* think about it . . . when you come to!' Cap swung his rife by the barrel and knocked the bald man into the middle of next Tuesday week while Ringo ducked the redhead's swishing club, came up inside the startled man's guard and lifted a knee brutally into his groin. The man gagged, dropped his billy and grabbed his willy, face contorted in agony. Ringo clubbed him to the ground.

Glass shattered above Ringo and a gun blasted. He dived left, taking the slower-moving Tyrell down with him. The older man grunted, lost his grip on his rifle. Ringo rolled on to his back, saw a hand with a smoking gun behind a top-floor broken window and fired two fast shots. One sent splinters flying: the other hit the man there in the shoulder, smashing the collarbone. They heard him screaming all the way as they rushed up the outside stairs where Ringo kicked in another door. The man was blood-spattered, writhing on the floor, and three sleepy whores gathered crumpled night attire around their weary and no doubt well-used bodies as they fled through an inner doorway.

Two more men appeared, one shooting as soon as he saw Ringo. He went down with a bullet through both legs, adding his screams to the man with the busted collarbone. Cap shot the gun out of the other's hand by a fluke.

Still, the bouncer was game and reached for a knife in his belt with his good hand. Ringo lunged for him, slashing with the rifle. The man yelled as he tripped and went backwards down the flight of stairs into the dim light of the rooms below where a couple of wall-bracket lamps still burned low. They were dully reflected by the bottles of liquor on the shelves behind a padded bar.

Ringo grabbed the two wounded men by their shirt collars after tossing his rifle to Cap. He went down the stairs ploddingly, the men groaning or shouting as they bumped alongside, step by step. He let them roll six steps from the bottom.

There were six or seven women clustered in one room, in various states of undress, looking scared. Big Lila herself, her main attributes mostly on show because of her hurried dressing when the shooting had started, glared and brought up a derringer, aiming at Ringo.

Cap lifted his rifle. 'Lila, them beauties must make some kinda top-heavy record but I been wondering since last night if they was real, or some kind of rubber blowups. Reckon they might bust if I fired?'

Her face darkened, but, as he cocked the hammer she swiftly dropped the derringer to the floor.'

'What the hell do you two think you're doing?'

'You owe us two hundred bucks,' Cap said. 'At least.'

'The hell I do! You had a good time last night!'

'Some was good,' Cap conceded. 'Waking-up wasn't.'

'You better get outa here while you still can. You think you're tough, but we got protection that covers half the Territory. There's people, *big* people, have an interest in our business. They won't take kindly to this roustin'.'

She jumped, even gave a little scream as Ringo's rifle started firing shot after shot until the magazine was empty. The liquor bottles on shelves behind the fancy bar shattered and leapt, spilling their contents explosively.

'Christ, man! You're crazy!'

Ringo had his sixgun in hand now. 'S'pose my next couple of shots broke those wall lamps? Oil ought to be mighty hot having burned all night. . . .'

Lila knew when she was beaten and held up a flabby hand. 'Two hundred, was it?'

'Cheap at the price,' Ringo assured her.

When they quit town about noon, Ringo and Cap were feeling mighty pleased with themselves.

But maybe they wouldn't have been if they had seen the message Lila wrote with a shaking hand in the railroad depot telegraph office. 'Get that off to Riverton, fast!' she ordered the telegraphist, slipping him a silver dollar.

CHAPTER 6

CARNEVAN

The gunshots echoed in a series of diminishing sounds, bouncing around the twisted canyon, wall to wall.

Ringo, standing in the shade of a tree, lit his cigarette as Cap got stiffly to his feet from a prone position in the stubble grass of a low rise, smoking Winchester in hand. 'How'd I do?'

'Clipped a couple branches, laid a scar or two on the trunk.'

Cap Tyrell looked disappointed. 'I never hit the target you drew with charcoal?'

'If you'd been shooting at a man, he'd be dead. Target gives you an aiming point is all. Plenty of lethal parts around a man's chest that'll stop him dead. Don't have to be square on.' Ringo exhaled. 'You don't need me showing you anything more, Cap – you're OK with a Colt. It doesn't take much to strip it down and you'll soon master that.'

'Well, that's some better. Figured I was gonna be a loser with these here firearms.'

Ringo's gaze was steady. 'You must've had some experience with revolvers in the war. What about percussions?'

'Yeah – Gunnison & Griswald, pretty damn near as good as this Colt, but I was a captain, remember. I wanted my guns cleaned or oiled, I just told someone to do it.'

Ringo held his gaze, then nodded slowly. *But before he became a captain Tyrell would have been working his way up through the ranks and must have had orders from officers to strip and clean* their *weapons. . . .*

'Eyes aren't what they used to be,' Cap said, breaking in on his thoughts.

'Get closer to your target.'

Tyrell smiled crookedly. 'Target I want is the Bosun – I don't figure to get too damn close to that son of a bitch.'

'You'd bushwhack him?'

'For damn sure!' There was belligerence in Cap's tone and his eyes held steady on Ringo's face, challenging him, perhaps, to fuss about it.

'As long as you nail him, huh?'

'As long as I nail him. Funny thing is, the bastard did me a favour of sorts, and don't even know it.'

Ringo waited in vain for further details. 'What makes you think he's in this neck of the woods?'

'Aw, after I got out, left the Pen, I looked up a couple men fellers inside had told me about. Every man Bosun had ever laid that lousy whip on was behind me, couldn't give me enough help to locate him. They asked around.' He paused, and Ringo was surprised to see Cap battling some sort of decision before he continued: was it how much to tell Ringo, even at this stage, after what they had been through together so far? There was something Cap wasn't quite sure about passing on to Ringo.

But Cap merely said, 'They found out there was a limey travelling around this area with a red bag – looking for work on the ranches. Said he was broke. It had to be the Bosun: the prison refused to pay him when they fired him. Carried that damn bag every-where and seems he'd took his whip to some civilian who happened to be the son of a Division Commander in the cavalry. That was s'posed to've happened way to the north, but he could've come south where there was more chance of getting away from Pappy.' He shrugged suddenly. 'I knew I'd need some money to buy more info, which is why I went after that gold on the island.'

'Well, we best start riding and checking out the ranches.'

'Ringo, don't get me wrong. I'm mighty obliged to have a man like you siding me, but – well, I can't really see why you're doing this.'

'You know damn well why.' Ringo let the words hang and for a moment thought Cap looked a mite worried. Then he added, 'You pulled me out of the river, and no matter what you say, I aim to square things with you – so I'll help you find the Bosun.'

'I meant it when I said I'll bushwhack the bastard!'

'Then you do it, if that's the way you have to get him, but I'll be there in case you run into any trouble.'

Tyrell nodded slowly. 'That's mighty good to know.'

But, somehow, he still sounded a little dubious. . . .

Ringo couldn't explore that aspect any further because three riders had appeared, two blocking the main entrance to the canyon, the other, a narrow side trail that led out of the tangle of rocks and draws.

All of them held rifles.

One was a woman.

The woman was guarding the single trail and tossed her head to get some of her flaxen hair out of her face as the warm breeze fingered through the draw.

'You're scaring my cattle with all that shooting.'

Cap took a step forward, halted abruptly as the two men cocked their hammers. 'Whoa, easy there! Was just target shooting, ma'am. Sorry, we didn't know there was any cows nearby.'

'Clean the wax outa your ears, old-timer,' said one of the men flatly, bald, bullet-headed, his hat hanging down his back by the tie-thong. 'I can hear 'em plain as you like.'

So could Ringo now. Cap nodded. 'Well, we never heard 'em before.'

'Too much damn shootin' goin' on. What we gonna do with 'em, Dale?' asked the tough ranny.

The girl lowered her carbine. 'Do? Nothing, Lem. What'd you expect to do with them?'

Lem shrugged. 'Trespassers – kick their butts off Square J at least.'

'Damn right!' The second man backed him up.

He was rangy, this one, had a drooping moustache and it was so straggly, Ringo was sure he was wearing it just to try to make himself look older. He was only a kid underneath.

The girl frowned at him, addressed Cap and Ringo. 'You two, this is my ranch land you're shooting up.' Her head jerked towards the rock wall at their back. 'There's a way out through there that'll take you to town.'

'Not going to town,' Ringo told her.

'You lookin' for one of the ranches?' Lem demanded suddenly. 'Like mebbe – Cross C?'

Cap started to say, 'Not unless—' but broke off as Ringo said a flat, 'No.'

Dale gave them a searching look before saying, 'Then I'll show you a trail that'll take you clear around my range – and you'd better use it. If you're found on my land again, Lem can do what he likes with you.'

The bullet-headed man grinned and spat. 'C'mon, gents, be a coupla sports. Tell us to go to hell!'

The young, moustachioed one chuckled. Dale's face remained sober, her eyes flashing at Lem.

'That's enough! Well? Are you going? Or merely going to argue?'

Ringo nodded to Cap and the man sheathed the rifle he was still holding. Both mounted. Lem looked disappointed.

'Just before we go, ma'am,' Cap said, as he started to turn his horse. 'You heard of a feller in these parts, a limey, who carries a red bag or keeps one in his bedroll?'

Dale frowned and the young rider snapped his head around to Lem. 'Bates had a red bag, didn't he? Recollect Bobcat seen it one day pokin' outa Bates's warbag, said it felt like it was full of dead snakes, Then Bates jumped him and kicked the b'Jasus outa him. Near killed him before they could pull him off.'

'And Chandler fired him on the spot,' Lem added, looking at Dale, 'Which is hard to swallow, seein' the kinda crew he uses at times, but it seems to be gospel. They even seen Bates off at gunpoint.' He glanced at Ringo and Tyrell. 'Friend of yours, this Bates?'

Ringo could see the girl was hanging on their answer and he said quietly, 'Never met the man.'

All gazes swung to Cap then. 'No friend – but I'd sure like to meet up with him. Who's Chandler?'

'My neighbour. Runs Cross C with a hardcase crew, but Bates was a bit too mean even for Chandler, I think. He's not all that bad, just tough and battling to make a go of his ranch.'

'Anyone know where Bates went?' Cap asked casually.

'He came to my place, looking for work,' the girl told him. 'But I didn't take to him.' She flushed a little as she added, 'He made me feel . . . queer.'

'Scared?'

That bought Ringo a cold look and her jaw lifted, jutting in a mild defiance. 'I said *queer*.'

'My question still stands,' Cap said with a touch impatience. 'Where's Bates now?'

'I have no idea,' Dale told him and glanced at her men. 'Lem? Jinx?'

Lem shook his head but Jinx said, after a short

hesitation, 'Cleary from the swing station up at Flagg said he got on a stage there, headed for Walnut Creek. But Pauley, one of the drivers, told me Bates got off at Yellowbank.'

'I told you to stay clear of that lot at Flagg, Jinx!' Dale snapped and the young rider tilted his head at her in almost the same way she had tilted hers at Ringo earlier.

'Judas, Sis! I'm twenty years old an'—'

'And until you turn twenty-one, you're my responsibility.'

'What's Yellowbank?' cut in Ringo.

Dale shot him an angry look at the interruption but said curtly, 'A place where they once mined sulphur – years ago, before there was any real settlement around The Tanks, and, of course, long before the railroad came.'

'It's a kinda meetin' place, too,' Lem added. 'Fellers headed for the outlyin' ranches sometimes get met there and taken out to whoever hired 'em. Trails fan out in all directions.'

'Then Bates could've been on his way to one of those ranches,' Cap thought aloud. 'How many are there?'

'Five or six – yeah, six.'

'You two aren't by any chance lawmen are you?' Dale asked suddenly.

'More like bounty-hunters,' opined Lem. 'See the way the young one wears his rig?'

'Wrong on both counts,' Ringo said. 'Cap has some business with a man answering Bates's description, that's all.'

'You goin' along to hold his hand?'

Ringo ignored Lem's sneer. 'Something like that. Cap, we best be moving.'

'Wait – ma'am, can you give us directions to this Yellowbank? And tell us something of the outlying ranches? I can pay you for your trouble.'

She stared at Cap and then shifted her gaze to Ringo. Lem and Jinx waited, the latter sort of expectantly with his lower lip sagging a little.

'They aren't . . . regular spreads out there. Not all of them. According to rumour they harbour men on the run and aren't averse to throwing a wide loop over the herds of legitimate ranches.'

'Like yours, ma'am?' Ringo asked casually.

'*Just* like my Square J,' she told him.

'Them spreads sound like the kind of place Bates might go to,' allowed Cap slowly. 'Still like to look 'em over.'

The girl nodded as if she had expected the answer. 'All right. It'll be near supper-time when we get back to the ranch. I can draw you maps or show you on the survey chart where these places are. It'll be best if you make an early start in the morning, too, because it gets hot mighty fast in those hills.'

'They stayin' over?' demanded Lem, and her eyes nailed him back in his saddle so that he murmured something under his breath.

'Mighty kind of you, ma'am,' Cap said. 'Ain't it, Ringo?'

The mention of the name brought Lem up with a start and he narrowed his eyes as he looked at Ringo, who ignored him and set his horse moving to follow the girl on the trail leading to the tangled draws radiating from the main canyon.

Lem somehow looked more pleased with himself, almost smiled as he nodded slowly, as if a puzzle had just been solved.

'You know him?' asked Jinx quietly, putting his mount alongside Lem's.

'No, but I seen him once, in El Paso. Between you an' me, kid, I wouldn't want my name to be Bates for all of the gold in Montezuma's treasure.'

It was the hardhead rancher named Chandler who met Dutch Carnevan when the pseudo sheriff stepped down from the train as the loco prepared to take on water at the high tanks. Dutch wasn't wearing his badge, but he did have a cotton pad held on by crossed tape covering his left ear.

'What happend to Big Lila?' Carnevan said, vaguely amused as he looked around at the crude siding. 'Thought from that wire she sent she might've been lookin' forward to seein' me.'

'You'd have to ask her – find her down at the Paradise, I guess. Or what's left of it after this Ringo and his sidekick got through.'

Carnevan's eyes narrowed. 'I ain't interested in his sidekick. Fact, thought I'd killed that old sunover out on the river island – Ringo's the one I want. And bad!'

'Well, word is they're lookin' for that crazy bastard of a limey I fired. Bosun Bates, he calls himself.' Chandler was a big man in his forties, with heavy features. He shook his large head. 'I've seen some tough rannies in my time but that one – Christ, the man's plumb loco. Never happier than when he's hammerin' someone's head in. Crippled two of my men and I figured that was two too many.'

'Hell with your crazy limey – it's *Ringo* I told you I want!' He touched the cotton pad covering his left ear.

'Yeah, I know, but if he's sidin' the oldster and the oldster's lookin' for Bates. . . .' Chandler let it hang and Carnevan nodded curtly.

'All right. Where's Bates now?'

'Not sure – now, wait up, Dutch! I've got men scourin' the country. He got off the stage at Yellowbank. Oughtn't to be too hard find where he went. He was flat broke so he'd have gone to one of the spreads up there, probably Handy's. We'll nail him down.'

'Better be fast.' Dutch stretched, easing the kinks from the journey up from Riverton on the hard, uncomfortable railroad seat. He touched his mangled ear again. 'I'm gonna cut Ringo's ears off before I shoot the son of a bitch. Well, we got a little time to kill, might's well go renew my acquaintance with Big Lila.'

Chandler smiled crookedly. 'Hope you're feelin' fit.'

'*She's* the one better be fit.'

Chandler looked a mite awkward as they started up towards town. 'Er . . . Dutch, if you could sorta wait a bit to see Lila? I forgot that Charley Gavin in the livery took care of Ringo and his pard after Lila's gals slipped 'em the Micky Finn.'

Dutch Carnevan stopped in mid-stride, hard face snapping around to the rancher. 'What're you gettin' at? C'mon, spit it out.'

Chandler tugged at an ear lobe. 'Charley kept their hosses and I thought he might have some idea where they was headed. Could be quicker than huntin'-up Bates.'

'You damn idiot! Why didn't you tell me first-up?'

Dutch changed direction, heading towards the livery with long, impatient strides. Chandler had to hurry to catch up. 'I got Mitch keepin' an eye on the stables.'

Carnevan didn't acknowledge this and walked straight past the lanky man lounging in the big double doorway, ignoring his greeting of, 'Howdy, Mr Carnevan, Gavin's workin' out back. Kid's shovel-lin' hay down the chute from the loft. . . .'

As Dutch kept walking the man let the words trail off and looked puzzledly at Chandler. The big rancher lifted a meaty hand in a placating gesture. 'Stay put, Cox.'

Gavin was forking hay into separate piles from a big untidy heap under the chute. A small amount came sliding down as Dutch and the rancher approached. Charley Gavin saw them, stiffened, a forkful of hay in mid-air. He read Carnevan's mood correctly and called up quickly to the kid working above, 'Jimbo! Go on home – *now!*'

'Pa?' the startled youngster asked, his dirt-smeared freckled face appearing at the top of the chute.

'*Go on home, dammit!*' shouted Gavin. 'Get the hell outa here!'

Mitch Cox lunged for the ladder leading to the loft, going up swiftly. Charley Gavin called again to the boy, spilling the hay from the fork and swinging towards Dutch and Chandler. They stopped as the livery man menaced them, awkwardly.

'C'mon, Charley,' Chandler said quietly. 'Don't be stupid, man. You know better'n this. Dutch only wants to ask a couple questions about that feller Ringo and the old man.'

The kid was yelling now and strands of hay came floating down through the cracks in the floorboards. Gavin's eyes were wild as he looked at Dutch.

'Aw, leave the kid alone! He dunno nothin'!'

'Didn't figure he would,' Carnevan said easily. 'But he might help jog your memory. Mitch! Send the kid down here.'

Jimbo yelled and next instant came sliding and tumbling down the chute, landing in an awkward heap. Gavin dropped the hay fork and ran to help the boy up. Carnevan was ahead of him, in two long strides, dragged the struggling, scared boy to his feet, squeezing one arm cruelly. He lifted him off the ground, kicking.

As Jimbo began to cry, Dutch drew his sixgun and pressed the muzzle against one of the bare dirty feet below the ragged edge of the soiled overalls. His bleak eyes were steady on Gavin's.

'If you know where Ringo went, Charley, you better damn well tell me – now! Or you're gonna have a cripple for a son.'

'Take it easy, Dutch!' Chandler said hoarsely.

Charley Gavin was a kind-hearted soul, but when it

came to choosing between his only son and a couple of friendly strangers he had helped – and who had even shown their appreciation in silver after they had wrecked the Paradise – it was no contest.

He told Dutch all he knew in one long, stumbling burst, interspersed with pleas not to hurt the writhing boy.

Carnevan nodded when Gavin had stopped speaking, and flung the boy towards his father who knelt swiftly, holding Jimbo tightly, stroking the tousled hair. Dutch took out a cheroot and fired up, watching.

'You're a good man, Charley, but you just got your sense of duty mixed-up. Best remember that. An' don't do it again.'

He stepped around the livery man and dropped the still burning match into the pile of hay.

'Judas priest! What the hell're you doin'!' Chandler was angry, but not *too* angry. Carnevan had a hold over him that kept him in line.

'Just so's he'll remember.' Dutch shifted his bleak gaze from Chandler to Gavin. 'You will, won't you, Charley?'

'Christ, Dutch!' Chandler said. 'This is a timber town and—'

'Shut up, Carey,' Dutch said, as Gavin rushed frantically for a pail and dived for the barrel of water at the end of the line of stalls – almost everyone of which held a horse.

Dutch kept walking, drawing deeply on his cheroot as the horses began to squeal and stomp in their stalls.

Choking smoke was pouring out of the rear of the long building when Dutch and Mitch walked through the wide front doors and on to the street. Chandler followed slowly, reluctantly. Then Carnevan hitched at his belt.

'Think I might go see Big Lila after all,' he said, giving the burning livery only a brief glance. 'That little session kind of got me all worked-up.'

CHAPTER 7

THE PAST

'That was an elegant meal, ma'am,' Cap Tyrell told Dale McMillan as he eased his chair back from the table with the checkered cloth. 'Best we've had for some time, eh, Ringo?'

'Best,' agreed Ringo.

The girl looked pleased – and different to when they had met on the range. She was wearing a gingham dress now, her hair piled up on her head neatly, held in place with a couple of Spanish combs. It made her look a lot more feminine than she had out at that canyon, cradling a Winchester.

'We can have coffee out on the gallery and watch the sun go down if you like.'

Cap was all for it although Ringo figured he had seen enough sunsets to last him the rest of his life. At the same time, he could appreciate the beauty of a western sky with endlessly changing colours and the

91

velvet night creeping in slowly to wipe them away. Until sunrise.

Ringo rolled and lit a cigarette and was surprised when the girl brought out a thin packet of cheroots, offered one to Cap.

'Guess I'm all through smokin', ma'am.' He coughed as if in some kind of explanation and she frowned slightly, took one for herself.

Ringo snapped a vesta into flame on his thumbnail and reached forward to hold it for her. She nodded, pale-blue eyes touching his face with mild amusement.

'I know – it's unusal for a woman to smoke. But I liked the aroma of cigars and cheroots so much as a child, when my father was home, that one day I experimented.' She waved the burning cheroot. 'Perhaps it was a mistake.'

'Just don't make a long habit out of it,' Cap advised. He coughed again for emphasis. 'Didn't do me any good.'

'You blame smoking for your cough?'

'That and the lousy damp cells and no warm clothes,' he said without thinking, suddenly breaking-off when he saw her startled face. He sighed. 'I spent some time in prison, ma'am – served it out. I ain't wanted by any law if that's what bothers you.'

She shook her head. 'It doesn't bother me.' She looked at Ringo, eyebrows arched, but didn't say anything.

He smiled thinly, shook his head. 'No. I haven't spent more'n a few days in local jails. Except once, in Mexico – dragged it out for a couple of months.'

'Well, I tend to take people as I find them. Their pasts are their own affairs.'

'Good attitude.'

She drew slowly on the cheroot. 'You'll be able to follow those rough maps I drew?' Both men nodded. She added quietly, 'I have no doubt you have a very good reason for looking for this Bates, who is a no-good, anyway, but I think I should warn you that the men who work and live out there beyond the Yellowbank are not friendly towards strangers. In fact, most of them are on the dodge. It's outlaw country. Most folk stay well clear of it.'

'Thanks for the warning, ma'am,' Cap said.

'But you're still going?' Her gaze travelled from Cap to Ringo and back to Tyrell.

'Have to.'

She looked at the silent Ringo. 'You *have to* go, too, Ringo?'

'I'm with Cap.'

She held his gaze for a few moments and then nodded slowly. 'I . . . see. Is it because you're friends, or have you hired out to him?' She flushed slightly, the colour heightened by the deep reddish glow of the burning sun as it sank quite fast now behind the ranges. 'I guess I shouldn't say this, but you look as if your gun might be for hire.'

Ringo didn't smile, kept his face blank. Cap kind of sniggered. 'Reckon he'd cost a lot more than I could afford to hire him! No, ma'am, he's one of them fellers lives by a code that's all his own and never mind anyone else. Figures I did him a favour and he aims to pay me back – whether I like it or not.'

Her face changed. The cheroot burned slowly between her fingers. 'Well, that's . . . that's quite a recommendation.' Still Ringo said nothing. 'I've caused you embarrassment, Ringo. I'm sorry. But I like to know about people. Running a ranch can become mighty boring after a time.'

'Guess I can savvy that. Doesn't bother me one way of t'other. I've hired out my gun at times, when I needed money bad. To both sides of the law.'

She dropped her eyes and busied herself stubbing out the cheroot which was only smoked halfway down. He thought the flush had deepened even more on her face but the light was fading fast now and he couldn't be sure.

She stood up. 'I'll have Esmeralda make up some grubsacks for you. They'll be with the maps on the parlour table in case you leave before I'm up and about.'

The men stood. 'Much obliged, Miss McMillan,' Cap said.

'You might as well call me Dale – most everyone does. The McMillan name's not used often around here. It's not one I care for – I sometimes use my mother's maiden name of Arliss.'

'You any kin to Hondo McMillan?' Ringo asked abruptly, and she looked at him sharply. 'Man I'm thinking of was a sheriff down in El Paso, few years back. You look a lot like him, got some of his mannerisms.'

After some obvious deliberation, she said soberly, 'I'm not flattered, Ringo, but Hondo was my father. I barely remember him. He walked out on my mother

94

and me, left us for another woman. Jinx was just a baby. My paternal grandfather left us this ranch after Ma died. You knew Hondo?'

Ringo nodded. 'Met him. Had no woman then. Fact seemed mighty lonely, pretty much unhappy.'

She waited and when he didn't elaborate said, 'Good. He was killed in a gunfight, I heard.'

'Yeah, some Mexicans and a couple of *gringos* tried to rob the Express office that was holding a payroll in transit. His deputy being out of town, guess he had no choice but to go up agin all four of 'em – he got 'em all, one of the *gringos* with his last bullet, as he was dying.'

Her face didn't change. She was silent for a time. 'I didn't know the details, just that he'd been killed.' He saw a glint of something damp in her eyes as night closed in. 'To be honest, I wasn't very interested. My mother died because of that man: forced to work so hard to support Jinx and me, she destroyed her health. I hold no fond memories of my father.'

'Well, they figure him for some kind of hero in El Paso. Town took up a collection, bought him a fancy marble headstone. It's worth seeing, if ever you're down that way.'

Her jaw tilted in that defiant way she had – the mannerism that had first made him ask if she was related to Hondo McMillan: he used to jut his jaw in the same manner.

Now, Dale turned away quickly, started towards the house. 'Thank you for telling me anyway, Ringo.'

When she had gone inside, Cap asked, 'That gospel?'

Ringo nodded gently. 'Yeah. I didn't *see* the gunfight, got back to town too late for that. They were clearing away the bodies when I rode in with my prisoner in tow.' His voice sounded bitter as he added, 'A drunk, who wasn't as drunk as he seemed: he'd busted a saloon mirror, clobbered the barkeep and a whore, stole a bottle of whiskey and made a run for it on someone else's horse. And I was green enough to fall for it, a wild goose chase to get me outa town. I went after him, just like he planned, left Hondo the only law in El Paso at that time.'

Cap's jaw dropped. 'The drunk was in on the robbery, huh?'

'The drunk, the saloon man *and* his barkeep.'

'And you were McMillan's deputy?'

'Temporarily, earning a few bucks to take me north. I chased that damn drunk all around the Border. Turned out he was the saloon-owner's son-in-law – even the horse belonged to the barkeep. And that's what kept me from being there when McMillan needed me.'

Cap shook his head slowly. 'You are something, Ringo. You have that look of a feller who's got something on his mind, slowly eating at him . . . wondered what it was.'

'Well, don't think you're all that smart,' Ringo told him shortly. 'Because if anything's bothering me, it's not that El Paso foul-up. That's long gone.'

Ethan Tyrell ran a tongue slowly around inside his lower lip. 'You know, when you get right down to it, I dunno hardly nothing at all about you, do I?'

'Mutual, Cap, mutual. Now let's find a bunk and

turn in. Gonna be a rough trail in the morning.'

On the way to the big bunkhouse, Cap asked quietly, 'What happened to that drunk and his father-in-law, and the barkeep? They quit town?'

'They tried.'

Cap waited. 'Well?'

'I had to stop 'em. *I* was the only lawman left. So I went after 'em, the saloon man, his lousy son-in-law and the barkeep who turned out to be something of a gunslinger.'

'Aaa-ndd?' Cap dragged out the word impatiently.

Ringo paused with his hand on the bunkhouse door latch, his face just visible in the dark. 'The town didn't buy them any marble headstones.'

They ate breakfast with the cowboys who were up before the sun anyway, preparing for the day's chores. While washing-up at the bench after rinsing their plates and mugs, Lem sauntered across, elaborately casual, rolling an after breakfast smoke.

'I seen you in El Paso once, Ringo.'

'I've been there a couple of times.'

'Five years back. One helluva gunfight in the Plaza del Sol. Three hardcases with guns, runnin' all over the place tryin' to get away from you – wreckin' market-stalls, upsettin' the greasers who owned 'em. You jumpin' from buckboard to wagon, even on to a roof chasin' one ranny. . . . He stopped, knelt down to draw a bead on you and you just kept on runnin' towards him, braced your carbine into your hip and blew him to glory. You'd think the poor son of a bitch was tryin' to fly, he was flappin' his arms so much when he went off the edge.'

Jinx had come up and his eyes were wide with excitement. 'Wooo-eeee! You really done that, Ringo?'

Ringo barely nodded, eyes on Lem. 'It was something had to be done, was all.'

'Sure. Everyone knew you'd been flim-flammed into leavin' the sheriff on his own.' Lem had a small audience of other cowpokes coming out of the bunkhouse now. But he paused before continuing, 'Funny, I didn't know his name was McMillan – everyone just called him Sheriff Hondo.'

Jinx straightened, sobering now, frowning at Ringo. Lem played up to his growing audience, looking kind of smug.

'The saloon man was the scared one, 'cause you'd already winged him. He was yellin' to his barkeep to nail you.' Lem looked around at the expectant faces. 'Barkeep had a sawed-off Greener and swung it on to Ringo here.' He shook his head briefly. 'Might just as well've put the barrel in his mouth and pulled both triggers and saved time.'

'Leave it at that.'

'Hell don't stop now, Lem!' urged young Jinx, moving his weight from one foot to the other in his growing excitement, but looking at Ringo in a strange, calculating way. 'I want to hear it all!'

Lem needed no urging, jerked a thumb in Ringo's direction. 'This ranny did some kinda shoulder-roll, clear off the roof, landed on his feet after crashin' through an awning over some Mex's geew-gaw cart. And I swear his hand was no more'n a blur, he worked that carbine's lever so fast. His first shell was still risin' from the breech when the next case kicked out, and a third, before the first hit the ground.' He laughed with a crooked smile. 'Fact, it hit about the same time as the 'keep. Dead as a plank.'

The cowboys murmured. Cap watched Ringo's face tighten, not at all pleased.

'What – what happened to the saloon man?' Jinx asked.

Lem and Ringo locked gazes. 'Will I tell 'em?'

'You seem to be the one doing all the talking.'

Lem nodded and was already speaking before Ringo had finished. 'That saloon man was so goddamn scared, knowin' a noose was waitin' for him, or twenty years in the pen at least if he gave up – well, he shot himself. Right there in the middle of El Paso with half the town watchin'. Lot of folk'll never forget that day, Ringo.'

'Me, neither. Now, we better ride, Cap. Long way to go,' He threw Lem a cold look and the cowboy seemed to shrink a little but gave a jerky grin and moved closer to the men who had been watching and listening.

Jinx seemed strangely sober now.

He stepped forward and it was clear he was going to ask for more details, but he stopped in his tracks when he saw the bleak set of Ringo's features. The cowboys seemed wary but respectful. Lem, feeling safe now in the midst of the others, looked like a cat that had just swallowed a canary: likely he wouldn't have to pay for his drinks for a week or more, telling and retelling the El Paso story in the Paradise Bar. . . .

Ringo didn't go up to the house to say farewell to Dale, but Cap did, picked up the final map she had been making for them and thanked her once again. 'Ringo says thanks, too.'

Her eyes went past Cap's shoulder. 'He must be tired.' At his quizzical look, she added, 'If he can't walk up here to say goodbye. Or is it just too much trouble for him?'

'He's kinda impatient,' Cap said lamely. He touched a hand to his hatbrim and folded the map and put it in his pocket. 'We're both obliged for all your help, ma'am. *Adios.*'

As he started back to where Ringo waited with the horses and the pack mule, she called quietly, 'If you come back this way, call in. You'll be most welcome, Cap.'

He waved and a couple of minutes later they rode out. She waited to see if Ringo would turn and wave and hid any disappointment she felt as Jinx came hurrying up.

'What's got you so excited? Has that gunfighter been filling your head with some of his wild stories?'

'Aw, he never said hardly a word, Sis, but Lem did. He seen Ringo in El Paso shootin' it out with them hardcases who'd been behind the Express office raid. One feller was so scared of Ringo he blew his brains out rather than face him.'

'That's enough! Lem ought to know better than to tell such stories!'

'Aw, Lem was there an' seen it. Ringo didn't want him to tell it. Thought he was gonna hit Lem.' He shrugged disappointedly. 'But he never. Sis, it must've happened right after Pa was killed after his deputy run off an' left him to fight the robbers all by hisself.'

Dale was pale now, her face tight and pinched. 'All right, Jinx, drop the subject, please!'

'Hell! Ringo must've been that deputy! Left Pa to tackle them robbers! Lem said as much!'

'Don't you cuss when you're speaking to me, young man! In fact, don't you cuss at *all* within my hearing, or you'll be eating off the mantelpiece for a week, your backside'll be so sore!'

'OK, OK! Don't be so da— so bossy!' Jinx pouted, not going to be diverted by her attempt to change the subject. 'Yeah, if Ringo was that deputy, run out on Pa, then when Pa was killed his conscience must've got the better of him and he tackled the fellers behind the robbery. Coulda happened that way, couldn't it, Sis?'

'Why ask me? I don't know. Anyway, it was a long time ago and our father chose the life he wanted to lead, left Ma to work herself to death, and you and me to make out as best we could. Whatever happened to him, was of his own making.'

Jinx looked suddenly stubborn. 'You always take on so about Pa, Dale!'

'Why shouldn't I? I shouldn't have to explain to you why I feel bitter about what he did. You ought to feel the same way!'

'Well, I don't! That painted woman who sweet-talked him into leavin' didn't last long, anyway. She run off with some rich Mexican *ranchero* he told me. He was just – weak, Sis. If Ma'd given him a chance when he wanted to come back that time. . . .'

Her eyes blazed and he stepped back hurriedly. 'Ma did right! You were too young to understand! Now I don't want to hear any more. Go and find some chores to do.'

'Huh! You're just jealous because I was the one he came back for! Said he wanted his son to be with him.' His smug manner drained away suddenly and he said in a quieter tone, 'But he liked you, too, Sis, I know from the way he talked about you. He was really sorry for leavin' us – and Ma.'

'He *kidnapped* you, Jinx! He didn't ask! He just took you, right out of your bed! Oh, I know he bribed you with fast talk and the promise of a pony of your own. I don't blame you. You were very young and—'

'I was old enough to know he really cared about me! You, too, I guess, but he figured it was best to leave you with Ma. He was good to me, Sis. Was only when you sent that tough ramrod we had at the time, Mooney, that things got rough. If Mooney hadn't slugged him when he wasn't lookin' and grabbed me—'

'I'm glad he did! You'd have nothing if you'd been left with Hondo McMillan! You wouldn't have had even the little education we managed to give you, or a part of this ranch to look forward to when you're older. You wouldn't've been cared for properly – you'd probably be *dead*!' She was becoming emotional and Jinx thought she was about to cry. But suddenly she got a hold of herself, forced a brief on-off smile and lightly cuffed the boy across the ear, bringing a howl from him out of all proportion to the hurt. Jinx was now looking for some way to ease back into his sister's good books. He had been unsettled by all this talk about the past and felt confused. Dale recognized this. 'Now go change that filthy shirt and you can drive me into town in the buckboard – I have some business with the cattle agent.'

That brightened Jinx no end and he skipped off towards the back of the house where he had his own room, yelling like a young Indian brave on his first pony-stealing raid.

Dale McMillan stood there on the stoop, watching the two dwindling riders through the dust their horses raised as they headed into the hills. She mused half aloud, 'I'm beginning to wish I'd never met you, Ringo. You've stirred up too much of the past. . . . *Too damn much!*'

CHAPTER 8

OUTLAW COUNTRY

They smelled the smoke long before they saw the grey-brown smudge in the sky, rising from the direction of Pothook.

Both could see the blackened scar at the northern end of town, still smouldering, as men moved about hurriedly, running back and forth with wooden buckets slopping water. A long, dark canvas hose stretched from the tanks, damp and leaking, like some huge Amazonian python, as men worked hand-pumps sluggishly, weary and near exhaustion.

'It's the livery stables,' Dale said quietly, her whole frame stiff with tension. 'Go on, Jinx! We can help!'

She clung to the sun-heated iron rail of the seat as the boy whipped up the team. Even people not actually residing in a town whose buildings were mostly made of wood, lived with the fear of fire way out here. Everyone knew the impact an out-of-control fire could have on a town: it meant no more essential supplies, no outlet for ranch goods, no jobs – except for the undertaker, maybe. After fire ripped through a timber town, recovery was always long and difficult.

As they swung on to the final approaches across the slopes where the high tanks were, Dale stood in the seat, shading her eyes.

'It's almost burned out now,' she said. 'The feed barn next door is scorched and the workshop of the freight depot at the back looks damaged. . . . But they seem to have it well under control, thank God. Not that it'll do poor Charley Gavin much good. He's lost his livelihood.'

Dale and Jinx joined the townsfolk in the bucket-brigade lines, dousing the last of the flames. They were told that almost all the horses had been saved, two dying in the smoke and one burned so badly Charley Gavin put it down on the spot. Once she knew no one had been seriously hurt, Dale asked how the fire started.

'Someone careless with a lighted match, far as we can make out,' she was told.

But another man who had been fetching his mount when the fire started, said quietly, making sure he wasn't overheard: 'I seen Dutch Carnevan and Carey Chandler in there, Mitch Cox, too. Dutch was shakin' up Charley's kid, shoutin' and cussin' – an' when Dutch left he had a new cheroot burnin'. You ask me, he was the one dropped the match.'

That would be exactly the kind of thing Dutch Carnevan would do if he lost an argument, or things hadn't gone the way he expected. Or if he wanted to teach someone a lesson. If Dutch was the culprit, it was no big surprise. But what bothered Dale most now was just what had brought Carnevan here in the first place – and being met by Carey Chandler seemed to indicate he had been sent for.

That was a combination that spelled no good for anyone in Pothook that she could think of.

But she had a hunch that Carnevan's presence had something to do with Ringo – or maybe Captain Ethan Tyrell. She had no real reason to think this, but sometimes her hunches just came out of nowhere and more often than she was comfortable with, they were proved right. She found it kind of scary, almost like she was part witch at such times.

The one man who could tell her, probably, was Charley Gavin. He would be busy now after losing his stables, but maybe he was also good and mad at Carnevan, in which case, this would be the best time to question him.

'Jinx, go to Emerson's Emporium and fill this order.' She handed him the shopping list she had written out back at the ranch. 'I'll be down at the cattle agency. Meet you outside Emerson's. Oh, if you finish early, you might see if you can help with the clearing-up here.'

Jinx didn't look too enthusiastic about that: grimy, sweating men worked in amongst the smoking, charred timber, as he drove off towards the general store.

Charley Gavin was harassed and impatient folk who weren't satisfied with having their mounts survive the fire, were demanding recompense for saddles and other riding gear they had stored at the livery.

'For Chris'sakes!' Gavin exploded. 'Give a man a chance! I've got some insurance comin'! I'll sort all this out when I'm paid – for now, just gimme some room!'

He turned away from the mumbling men, stopped when he saw Dale. 'You never had no stock in here, did you, Dale?'

She shook her head, took his arm, led him away to a leaning charred wall of some half-burned stalls and offered him a cheroot. He took one and she lit both, Gavin involuntarily jerking his head back as the match flared.

'I ain't gonna enjoy this!' he gritted, rolling the burning cheroot between his fingers. At her quizzical look he added, 'Dutch Carnevan lit one and dropped his goddamn match into my hay pile. Just because I helped Ringo and Cap after they were Mickey Finned at the Paradise.'

It was what Dale wanted to hear and she sympathized and soon had him talking. Her hunch that Dutch was here in relation to Ringo was quickly confirmed.

'D'you know where Carnevan and Chandler went?'

He started to shake his head. 'Too damn busy tryin' to beat out the fire to notice – no! Wait! Dutch wanted to go see Big Lila. Guess Chandler went with him.'

'I meant where they went, Charley: out of town. Did they go after Ringo?'

'Had the notion they would . . . Dale, I got a slew of work to get through.'

'I'm sorry to delay you, Charley. If you need help, I can leave Jinx with you for a while?'

'I'll have plenty of helpers.' There was an edge of bitterness in Gavin's tone. 'Look at the sons of bitches! Turnin' over everythin' to see what they can find – and keep!' He strode off, yelling at a small bunch of looters – not all scavenging kids, but some adults too. 'Come on! Get to hell outa here, you bunch of goddamn vultures. . . .'

Like most ranchers whose spreads were some distance from town, Dale always carried saddles and warbags in the buckboard. If a wheel broke on the way to or from town instead of being stranded, the team could be saddled and ridden to get help. In this country, with water concentrated in relatively tight areas, it paid to be able to get to help as soon as possible. More than one man or woman had died trying to walk out, not realizing how hard water was to come by away from the river.

So, with Jinx already back, the packages containing the stores roughly stowed in the buckboard, Dale told him to saddle the horses. 'Where we goin', Sis?'

Soberly, she said, 'We're going to try to catch up with Ringo and Cap – Dutch Carnevan and Chandler are after them, but we can cut across country and get ahead with a little luck.'

Jinx whistled softly, glad they had rifles in the back of the buckboard, too. He was excited, but there was a kind of churning in his belly as well.

Carnevan and Chandler – two of the toughest men in all of the South-west.

Although – maybe Ringo was right up there with them.

Maybe.

Neither Ringo nor Cap Tyrell liked Yellowbank. It had a few shacks on the slopes, but the rocks were dark and mostly streaked or dusted with yellow remnants of the sulphur that still lay in unworked deposits. The slopes behind the shacks showed several yawning entrances to mine tunnels, yellow again splashed around the edges, looking like holes left by rotten teeth in diseased gums.

There was no one outside the shacks, but both men saw rags of curtains move as their arrival was observed. Behind the largest shack were corrals that needed repairing, a dozen or so horses standing desultorily under the dubious shade of a brush shelter.

'Bet the stage changes teams quick as they can in this place,' observed Cap, coughing violently and spitting.

Ringo frowned slightly: he figured Cap's cough was getting worse since the soaking back at the river island. The older man's cheeks were sunken and grey, with a couple of bright red high spots. He could be heading for a fever.

'You better watch that cough.'

Cap squinted. 'You beginning to sound like a bit of an old woman, friend.'

'Just trying to keep you alive a little longer.' Ringo smiled faintly. 'Till we find this Bosun.'

Cap smothered another bout of coughing, fist

covering his mouth, shoulders and thin body shaking with the effort. 'Reckon he ain't here, anyways,' he managed to say between coughs.

'We can ask.' Ringo nodded upslope where three men had appeared, one from the stageline shack, the other two from one of the other tumbledown structures. They all held guns, the stageline man with a sawn-off shotgun, the others hefting Colt pistols.

'Who are you and what d'you want?' called the stageline agent, short hair awry as if he had just been aroused from a daytime sleep, but holding the shotgun steady.

'Looking for a pard of ours passed this way recently, so we're told,' Ringo said, hands folded on his saddlehorn. Cap sat slouched, one hand close to the butt of his rifle where it protruded from the saddle scabbard.

'He got a name? This – pard – of yours?'

'Calls himself Bosun – a limey.'

The short man spat and the other two seemed to tense. 'That son of a bitch! Owes me for booze and a bed! You feel like settlin' his debts?'

'Feel like settling *him*,' answered Cap.

The short man grinned abruptly. 'Not such a good friend after all, huh? You don't look like law, but I ain't sure about your pard there.'

The trio gave Ringo their attention. He returned their stares unworriedly. 'No call to get insulting, *amigo*.'

The short man half-smiled, wary still, but noting Ringo's easy confidence and the way he wore his gun.

'Just like to know who met him,' Cap said calmly.

110

'Then we'll be on our way.'

The three Yellowbank men exchanged glances. One of the two from the tumbledown shack, swarthy, broken-nosed, asked, 'You wouldn't be willin' to pay for information, would you?'

'Right first time. We're bust.' Cap gestured vaguely to somewhere beyond the depressing hills. 'Heard there're spreads out there who pay good, though.'

'Depends on a man's talents.' The swarthy man liked that and grinned at his companions, but they remained sober. 'And how about this limey – you meetin' up with him?'

'Sure would like to,' Cap told him. 'But we won't be shakin' his hand.'

'They're law, Skeets,' growled the third man, bigger, healthier and more beard-shaggy than the other two. 'Law – or bounty hunters.'

Skeets, the stageline rep., glanced sharply at the speaker, then swung his eyes back to Ringo and Cap. 'That limey got a bounty on him?'

'He oughta have – but far as I know there's no dodger out for him.'

'You'd say that anyway,' the bearded man said.

'Guess I would – but happens to be gospel. Ringo, I think we're wasting time here.'

'Yeah,' Ringo agreed, and the sounds of three shots rolled across the stark hillside, spurts of dirt streaked with yellow exploding around the boots of the three men.

They danced involuntarily, staggering and stumbling. Skeets, highest on the slope, lost his footing and skidded forward, the shotgun sliding out of his grip. The bearded man managed to right himself and brought up his Colt swiftly, eyes deadly. He jerked back violently as Ringo shot him through the gun arm, cannoning into his pard who was trying to use his own pistol. As the bearded man dropped to his knees, sobbing, grasping a blood-spurting arm, his companion hurriedly lost his gun and grabbed a handful of the throat rasping air. Skeets sat there cursing as he looked at his gravel-scarred hands which were bleeding slightly.

Cap levered a shell into the rifle he now held.

'Now, about this limey,' he said conversationally.

They rode over the crest of the depressing hillside and stopped in the shade of a cleft boulder to look at the maps Dale had drawn for them. Cap shuffled through the four pages, stopped and went back to map number two.

'This one I reckon. See? She's written in the names of the spreads in the area she's drawn – Handy's place is here.' He snorted as one gnarled finger with dirt under a horny nail tapped the flimsy paper. 'Look at the position! Smack in the middle of miles of brush with draws and canyons all around it! And a trail to the state line or Indian territory no more'n a frog's leap away! Widelooper's heaven!'

Ringo nodded. 'Or a good place to stop over for a man on the run before crossing the tine.'

'Well, like I told them fellers at Yellowbank, far as I know Bosun don't have any dodgers out on him, but could be one since I last seen the son of a bitch.'

'Or he's just running scared – we might not be the

only ones after him.'

'Hey! That's possible! He must have more enemies than Geronimo.'

'Then we better get moving.'

Cap nodded and started coughing again. Ringo frowned.

He hoped Bates would still be at Handy's spread as Skeets had reluctantly told them back at Yellowbank, for he had a feeling Cap wasn't going to last long in this rough outlaw country.

Age and twenty-five years of prison diet and ill-treatment had sapped Tyrell's strength. It would be a pity if it gave out altogether before he had a chance to settle his scores with Bosun Bates.

The horses were better working as a team pulling a buckboard than carrying riders.

This was the conclusion Dale McMillan had come to after a long troublesome ride out from Pothook. Although they hadn't seen any sign of Carnevan and Chandler, riding with one of the latter's hardcases, Mitch Cox, she felt they must have lost ground because of the black she was using.

Jinx's mount, Rosie, was co-operative enough but her gelding, named Black Tom, was skittish and diffi-cult.

'You sure Tom had his sportin' tackle trimmed, Sis?' Jinx asked after a particularly prolonged bout of bucking and a display of bad temper by the black gelding. 'You ask me, he's likely to try an' jump Rosie if he gets the chance.'

Dale was some time replying as she fought the

113

rolling-eyed black, finally cuffed it with the rein ends. It shook its head, whistling angrily, but when the leather slapped down again across one ear, Tom decided to let Dale think she was boss – for the time being.

But there had been several occasions since leaving Pothook with Black Tom trying to prove his dominance. Dale was worried that they had dropped too far behind Carnevan so that her original plan of taking a shortcut to Yellowbank was now useless.

'How about I ride on ahead, Sis? I could make up some of the time we've lost. I stick around and have to wait for you to settle down old Black Tom every few minutes, we're gonna be still ridin' when the first snow hits.'

He was right, of course, but she didn't want to separate. 'Let's ride to that ridge and see if there's any sign of Carnevan,' she compromised.

For once, Black Tom behaved and they made the ridge top in a few minutes. She swept the rugged country slowly with her field-glasses. She pointed, offering Jinx the glasses. 'A thin smudge. I think it's dust, but it's very hard to see against the glare of the sky . . . just above that short line of sawtooths.'

Jinx found it easily enough. 'It's dust, I reckon, Sis, but if it is, we ain't never gonna out-run Carnevan from here. Not with Black Tom, leastways.'

'If it is Dutch and Carey Chandler.'

'Well, it won't be Ringo and Cap. They should be well into the rimrock country by now.'

'Let's hope so.' She looked again through the glasses, lowered them and turned to her brother. 'Do you think you can cut across, get ahead, and try to catch up with Ringo? But I mean just that, Jinx: forget Dutch, warn Ringo.'

He patted the neck of the sweating horse. 'Rosie's a good old gal – she'll bust a bellyband tryin'.'

Soberly she studied the country: this seemed the best solution, although the one she least wanted. 'All right! No more talk. Just do what you can, Jinx, and if you think you won't be able to warn Ringo in time, then make sure Carnevan doesn't see you.'

He was already spurring away and she watched, lifted a hand in a wave, teeth tugging at her lower lip.

Why am I doing this for a man I hardly know and don't even like very much?

She had no ready answer so touched her spurs to the black and lifted the reins.

Of course, Black Tom decided to act-up – simply by refusing to move. And Jinx was already out of sight. Now she was alone in outlaw country.

CHAPTER 9

BUSHWHACK

Ringo knew with a sickening feeling that they were lost.

Somewhere they had taken a wrong turning – and no wonder. The map Dale had copied from the last Ordnance Survey, a few years ago, in 1879, fairly wriggled with draws and canyons. Some probably were only roughly marked, showing twists and turns, and the transfer to paper from the survey figures would merely be an indication, rather than an inch-by-inch rendering.

'There're no signs of any brush, Cap,' Ringo said, turning his mount and riding down the slope to where the sick old man was huddling close to the small camp-fire they had built. 'This can't be the way to Handy's.'

Moments before Tyrell had been opening his shirt and rolling his sleeves as high as they would go on his arms, sweat running down his gaunt face. He had a fever but wasn't about to let it stop him now he was this close to running Bosun Bates to ground.

Ringo dismounted and took over the chore of making the coffee. He unstrapped his bedroll and removed a blanket, draping it about Cap's trembling shoulders. The man wheezed his thanks, backing it with a jerky nod of acknowledgement.

'You really need to see a sawbones, Cap.'

'I'll see one – after I see Bosun ... dead.' He coughed, a wet sound rumbling out of his chest. 'Don't look so worried, brother. I-I've had bouts like this for years. It'll pass.'

'Long as it doesn't take you with it when it does.'

'Cap'n Cheerful! Just what I need!'

Ringo shook his head, handed him a mug of steaming coffee and Cap wrapped both leathery hands around it. While he waited for his own coffee to cool, Ringo studied the map they had been using.

'Hell! Now I see it! Look, Dale's copied this faith-fully enough, but it doesn't show a complete canyon. There's some sort of creek crossing the end. The way it's drawn, it looks like a continuation of the canyon wall but I can see it's not now. We're too far to the east for any of these canyons to take us to Handy's.'

'Take your word for it,' Cap said, teeth chattering, spilling some coffee. 'Ringo, I-I guess I better rest-up some. Sorry I got you into this, but—'

'I'm here because I want to be here. Lie back against this rock and I'll drape the blanket over you. I recognize those trees yonder. We can stew up some of the leaves and resin from the trunk. Not exactly nectar of the gods, but you can drink it for your cough – even rub your chest with a handful of leaves, let the oil penetrate. It'll ease your breathing. Indians use it a lot on their kids.'

'Said you was getting to be an old woman before. Take it back. You know more about frontier living than I do. Seem to've forgotten that kind of stuff, if I ever knew it.'

Ringo frowned. 'Guess you had other things on your mind in jail all those years.' *But Cap had told him he had worked in the prison sick bay.* Right now, Cap looked uncomfortable and ran a trembling hand over his face.

'I dunno – mind's all kinda – mushy.'

Ringo nodded slowly, allowing this could well be caused by the fever, but it seemed to be just one more inconsistency in what Captain Ethan Tyrell had told him about himself.

And this was a hell of a time to start doubting the oldster.

He was collecting the tree balsam, Cap dozing against the rock, huddled in two blankets now, when he heard the gunfire.

It was echoing wildly because of the serpentine canyons and gulches and he couldn't tell where it was coming from, or how close it was to their camp.

Jinx McMillan had pushed Rosie too hard.

The mare was a powerful animal but the chunky muscle development was better suited to working between the shafts of a buckboard than stretching in a long lope with a rider in the saddle.

Jinx sensed the power in the mare under him and used rein ends and the occasional rake of spurs to urge it on. She didn't care much for the touch of the spur rowels and Jinx didn't want to cut her flanks up, but he felt he was being entrusted with a mighty important chore and so was harder on Rosie than he would be normally. He bullied her up some of the rugged slopes, almost spilled from the saddle on one steep grade, Rosie whickering and snorting, fighting for a foothold.

Angry, he let his temper get the better of him and whipped and gouged until the mare fought back in the only way she knew how.

She deliberately rolled halfway up a grassy slope, belly close to the ground, humping her back briefly and catching Jinx off-guard. He hit lightly enough – he wasn't very heavy in any case – began to slide, grabbing at anything that might slow him down. The grass pulled out under his grip and then he hit a bare slope, the gravel tearing at his clothes, dust boiling around him.

When he stopped, he had gravel scars on elbows and one hip, trousers and shirt torn. His sixgun had fallen from the holster and he limped back up the slope to get it, swearing. Rosie was standing serenely, higher up now, looking down, reins hanging. He picked up a stone, ready to hurl it, but suddenly grinned and dropped the missile.

'You bitch! You got me that time – but I guess I deserved it.' He plodded on up and the horse began to back away a foot at a time, staying just beyond his reach. His smile disappeared. 'Aw, *hell*! Don't start that, Rosie! No! No – wait-up – come here, dammit!'

He was soon breathless chasing the horse: the

mare seemed to be enjoying herself, as he stumbled and scampered and when he had no breath left to even curse, she stopped and waited for him to reach her. The big brown eyes were wary and he knew if he made a wrong move now, Rosie would turn and run and leave him afoot in this dangerous country.

A second later, he found out it was even more dangerous than he had figured.

There was a sudden eruption of gravel a foot below where he stood and almost at the same instant, he heard the crack of the rifle that had fired the bullet. Jinx reacted by pure instinct, threw himself behind a low line of boulders and belly-crawled towards Rosie who was standing still with ears erect now, deciding her next move.

He glanced downslope and saw the riders, one man with a smoking rifle levering as he sat his saddle. A big man he recognized as Mitch Cox. Behind him he saw Carey Chandler unsheathing his Winchester. The third man had to be Dutch Carnevan: there was a white patch over his left ear.

Jinx swallowed, his tongue seeming to stick to the roof of his suddenly dry mouth. Three of the toughest hardcases in the territory and they were coming after him with guns blazing. He suddenly lunged upright, bony legs working like pistons as he lifted in a rolling dive over the rocks, landing beside the startled mare. Rosie snorted, jumped away and tried to turn at the same time. It resulted in a stagger and Jinx managed to grab the flying reins. He vaulted into the saddle as half-a-dozen bullets raked the slope, two ricocheting from the boulders, rock chips spraying. He wheeled the horse and felt her shudder, right foreleg collapsing briefly as a bullet gouged her hide.

He yanked upwards on the reins. 'Come on! Get – up!'

The action threw him about wildly but actually saved his life as the rifles kept thundering and lead buzzed about him. Jinx, heart hammering, threw himself along the mare, urging her to the gallop. He had his sixgun in his hand and without turning or looking, stretched his arm behind and triggered three shots downslope.

It might throw the others off briefly: he knew he wouldn't hit any of the trio except by a huge fluke, and that kind of thing didn't happen to anyone with the nickname of Jinx, even if it wasn't entirely deserved.

'It's the McMillan kid!'

He didn't know who yelled out, but he felt a coldness clutch at his heart now that he had been recognized.

'Bring him down!'

He knew *that* voice: Dutch Carnevan.

Two rifles fired several ragged shots and just as he urged Rosie over the crest he felt the mare shudder and start to fall away beneath him.

Then he sailed over her head and the hard ground rushed up to meet him in a hard, red explosion of pain.

Dale McMillan had dropped a long way behind, thanks to Black Tom. But at least she could see the mount was tiring of toying with her and she had now decided to stifle her irritation and impatience. Strangely enough, making her riled seemed to amuse the gelding and spur it on to misbehaving even worse than previously.

It took quite an effort, but she suddenly realized that by trying to ignore his antics, simply waiting for the conclusion and then letting the horse move along at its own pace, Tom started to settle down.

He had certainly expended a lot more energy than she had and finally they were making progress. But she was a long way behind Jinx now and couldn't see a dust trail, or even the remnants of one.

She knew she would have no hope of overtaking her brother. She had been born and bred to hardship and survived by determination and self-sufficiency, but she still felt apprehension, exposed as she was in this desolate land, and knowing unscrupulous men like Dutch Carnevan were loose in it somewhere out there.

Carey Chandler, she wasn't afraid of – she knew him to be a tough-minded rancher who ruled his spread with hard fists – but rumour had it that he was in debt to Carnevan and so at a disadvantage, having to keep on Dutch's good side – if he had one, which she doubted. But basically she thought Chandler had a decent streak in him. Cox was rumoured to be Dutch's man, one-hundred per cent, keeping an eye on Chandler.

Maybe she was fooling herself, but she clung to the notion Chandler wasn't a killer, finding some comfort in it as she rode on into the sun's glare.

Occasionally she touched the butt of the carbine in the saddle scabbard.

None of it did much to lessen her anxiety about Jinx. Then she hauled rein abruptly, bringing a head-shaking whinny of protest from Black Tom. Absently, she *shooshed* him, half standing in the stirrups, ears straining.

There was no mistake: she thought she had heard some dull plops, like a distant carpenter at work, hammering nails. But she knew what the sounds really were.

Gunshots – coming from the direction Jinx had taken.

Naturally, when she tried to get Tom started again, the gelding stood stubbornly still, like a statue carved in polished ebony. Immovable.

She almost wept with frustration.

Ringo rode with his rifle across his thighs, picking his way down a stone-studded slope that led into a skirt of grey brush, gradually thickening as it spread away into the distant hazy hills.

Somewhere out there, in a dip between the small rises, he knew Reed Handy's spread sprawled. He hadn't been able to find out much about Handy except that he was generally reckoned to be a wide-looper who shoved rustled stock over the state line or sold them to men from the fringes of the Badman's Territory. Others reckoned he made his living by hiding out men on the run, allowing them to lie low on his spread until they were ready to make a dash across the line where only a Federal warrant would have any effect.

Cap Tyrell followed, but about a quarter-mile back, sagging and rocking in his saddle. Ringo had wanted to leave him at their camp, but the oldster insisted on coming along.

'Apart from the whipping frame, this is the closest I've ever gotten to that son of a bitch, an' I don't aim to sit on my ass when I could be sighting down my rifle barrel at him.'

The gasping sentence had been followed by a bout of coughing and Ringo, though worried, felt this could be Cap's last chance to square with Bates. If he died doing it – or even attempting it – at least Cap would die happy.

Ringo still hadn't figured out just where the shooting had come from, but he decided to follow a hunch and make for Handy's – after all, that was supposed to be Bates's destination.

He hauled rein and turned slightly in the saddle at a raspy, cough-punctuated call from Cap Tyrell.

'Ringo . . . look . . . yonder.' Cap pointed with a shaking arm and Ringo shifted his gaze in that direction and saw a faint smudge of dust rising over the brush.

He spurred his mount to the top of a low rise, rose in the stirrups, then, sliding the reins to their limit, stood up on the saddle itself. He balanced precariously, using the taut reins for support, the horse not liking the shift in weight, or the concentration of it now in the small area of Ringo's boots pressing on its back.

Ringo almost toppled, managed to swing and

spread his legs, using thigh pressure to ease the speed of his drop. The jar hurt but not badly: mostly he felt a few stabs of pain through the groin and the base of his belly. But he had seen what he wanted to before he had been forced down.

'Cap, looks like three riders – could be dragging something behind. Didn't really have time to see what properly before I almost lost balance.'

'Must be Dutch Carnevan,' Cap wheezed, ranging alongside now. His breathing sounded like a leaky bellows. 'That's the general direction of Handy's over that way.'

Ringo nodded a mite absently: he was listening but part of his mind was elsewhere. He stiffened suddenly.

'Cap, I reckon those riders were dragging a man on the end of a rope behind 'em! I saw just a flash – but you know how sometimes a quick sighting will sort itself out into a definite image without you consciously thinking about it?'

'Who was it?'

'Didn't see enough detail – just someone stumbling along, fell once, not a big feller. But, whoever he is, if that's Carnevan leading, the poor devil's in big trouble.' Ringo listened to Cap's cough and hawking. 'You better stay put. I can—'

'You can go to hell, that's what you can do! *Bates* ain't a big feller – broad like a keg, but short. If they've got him hog-tied, that suits me.'

'Don't think this one was all that broad. . . .' But there was no sense in arguing – and no time. 'Cap, you'll have to try to choke off that goddamn cough!

125

It'll give us away if you don't.'

Tyrell looked briefly angry but he knew Ringo was right. He nodded jerkily, and unsheathed his rifle, levering a shell into the breech by way of answer.

That was good enough for Ringo and they rode warily through the brush, trying to keep down the dust of their passing so as not to alert the men ahead.

Whoever the prisoner was, it was a cinch he would be already marked down for torture or death by Dutch.

No sense in hurrying the poor devil's fate along unnecessarily.

But if it *was* Bosun Bates then it was only right that Tyrell should get first shot at him.

Literally.

CHAPTER 10

TRAIL MEET

Ringo dismounted at the base of one of the highest boulders in the clump and, holding his rifle, made his way through to the front. Heat blasted back at him from the rocks and he wiped sweat from his brow as he hunkered down in a patch of shade and tried to focus his glare-aching eyes.

He and Cap, who was now dismounting shakily at the other side of the boulder clump, had managed to glimpse the spreading brush and saw where the trail was. This was easy to tell: all they had to do was look for a thinning of the brush and that would indicate where riders had been in the past.

Once they saw how it wound in a meandering curve, following the natural contours of the ground, Ringo had led the way through to the boulder clump which rose above the grey-green thickets. Here they were actually ahead of the trio who were following the trail as the path of least resistance, but which took them away from the boulders, until it swung back in a tight arc, passing close below.

Cap was wheezing but seemed to have his coughing under control as he came up and flopped on the ground beside Ringo.

'OK?' All Cap could do was nod as he fought to settle his breathing, heart hammering wildly in his chest. 'They ought to show in a few minutes, about where that bush with the yellow flowers is. Not the one with the drooping flowers, the other where it looks like they're still in full bloom.'

'Kinda . . . far.'

'Easy rifle shot. You want to try for Bates? If it is him? Or you want me to knock down a couple of horses and pin 'em down?'

'Sure would . . . admire to get Bosun in my sights . . . but I'm jumping like a *cantina* whore. Think I can remember. . . .'

Ringo smiled, giving his attention to the bush with the yellow flowers now. Dust was spiralling from behind it and it would be only a matter of minutes before the first rider appeared.

'Damn! It's Dutch Carnevan, all right! Still got that patch over his ear. Hope it's painful. The big feller must be Chandler and the last one has the man at the end of the rope. Ooops! Fell again on his face. Climbing up.' He hissed an expletive. 'Hell! It's Jinx!'

Cap jerked, surprise swiftly giving way to disappointment. 'The hell's he doing with—?'

'Guess he doesn't want to be there! Face is a mess and his clothes are all torn. Been dragged quite a few miles by the look of it – kid can hardly stay on his feet.'

'Well, what the hell you waitin' for? Shoot that Carnevan bastard!'

Ringo hesitated. 'I've never bushwhacked anyone, Cap, I like the chances to be tolerably even. Way I was brought up.'

'Aaah! Kid'll be dead before you throw a loop on that conscience of yours!' Cap growled, bringing up his rifle.

'Dammit, Cap! Wait! I'll shoot Dutch's horse—'

Tyrell's rifle whipcracked but he was shaking so badly he missed Dutch, the man swinging instinctively to one side, as the lead hummed past.

'Boulders!' shouted Mitch, pointing. He had the rope leading from the staggering Jinx McMillan dallied round his saddlehorn. 'Two of 'em!'

Chandler was fighting his skittish horse now, his sixgun blasting in a few shots that could only have been meant to divert the bushwhackers. Cap triggered again and Dutch's horse's rump whipped violently as lead seared the hide. Carnevan went with the twisting motion and dived from the saddle, dragging his rifle with him as he hit and rolled under a bush. Chandler spurred away, leaping his mount over a low line of brush, crashing on through heavier foliage out of sight.

Ringo put two shots into the swaying brush, then swung his rifle towards Mitch Cox. The man deliberately jammed his spurs into his horse and the animal shrilled in protest, but gathered itself and lunged away. The rope snapped taut and Jinx McMillan was jerked roughly off his feet. He twisted and rolled at the end of the rope, crashing headlong through the brush, trying to use his bound hands to protect his already scratched and bloody face. His rangy body bounced and spun. If he yelled, the sound was lost in the crackling of brush, the clatter of hoofs and the spasmodic rattle of gunfire. He disappeared into the swaying, trampled bushes. Cox quit saddle, allowing his horse to race on, Jinx being dragged helplessly at the end of the rope.

'Christ! This is a mess!'

'Sorry, Ringo, thought I had a good . . . bead. . . .'

They both ducked as lead raked the boulders, ricocheting dangerously with snarling sounds. Dutch Carnevan lifted, fired, dropped, all in the space of an indrawn breath. The lead sprayed rock dust over Ringo's hat. Cap tried to shoot back but fumbled the rifle's lever. Chandler's lead tore the old man's hat off his head. He fell flat, dropping the rifle.

Then Dutch yelled, 'I got you spotted, Ringo, you son of a bitch! You shoulda made sure of me with that first shot, feller!'

'Plenty more where that came from, Dutch!'

'Then you better shoot 'em into the air! 'Cause any come my way, I'll blow this kid's head off! Or mebbe I'll start with his big toe and work my way up. You get the idea?'

'Would he?' wheezed Cap and Ringo nodded without hesitation.

'He's mean enough to – Cap, you're not in this. *No*! Damn you, listen! I'm the one Dutch wants. I can't let him kill Jinx. The kid's got nothing to do with it. You lie low. I'll go down there. While I'm doing it, they'll be watching me. Get on your hoss and make a run for it – *Christ! Will you listen!* Just get the hell away from here. Forget about the Bosun for now and save your own hide.'

'You got about one hundredth of a second, Ringo!'

Ringo, still glaring at Cap, stood quickly, lifting his arm and throwing his rifle well away from him.

'I'm coming, Dutch! Don't harm the kid!'

Dutch laughed. 'Who me? Aw, I'm hurt that you'd even think I'd be that mean, Ringo!'

'Comes from knowing you so well – I'm coming down.'

'And just keep comin' slow – dragging your fingers across the sky. Thaaaat's it! You can tell that old sourdough with you he can vamoose – we got no argument with him. But he stays, and he stays for keeps, watchin' the grass grow from underneath.'

Ringo turned his head slightly. Cap was easing back in the brush, but he was moving so that he would pass close to his dropped rifle.

'Don't, Cap! Just make a dash for it – you'll be out of range by the time Cox or Chandler can run up the slope to draw a bead on you. I'll delay 'em if I can.'

Cap ignored Ringo, drew his Colt and, staying low, thrust it through the brush, out of sight of the men below. He tossed it almost at Ringo's feet. 'When he asks for your sixgun, give it to him.' A cough caught Cap unawares and the brush where he lay shook briefly. Mitch Cox fired. Cap grunted and flopped back.

131

Ringo dropped quickly. 'Cap! You hit?' At the same time he scooped up Tyrell's Colt and rammed it into his belt at the back.

A bullet tore through the brush and twigs and leaves stung his face. He straightened quickly, empty hands in the air.

'Damn you, Dutch! You didn't have to shoot him! He was going.'

Carnevan laughed. 'Good shootin', Mitch! Give that man a cee-gar, Carey!' Then his voice hardened. 'Come on, Ringo! I'm all through playing! Get on down here and quick, or that old coot's gonna have company on his way to hell!'

Plodding, not looking towards Cap, Ringo picked his way carefully down the slope, delaying as much as he dared. He made his way towards the bushes where Dutch, Chandler and Mitch Cox waited.

Jinx McMillan lay on the ground, bloody and unmoving.

'Well, now, ain't this cosy?' Dutch Carnevan said, baring his teeth. 'The stuff of dreams!' He stepped forward and slashed at Ringo's face with his gun barrel. Ringo jerked back, felt the wind of its passing. 'All right! I'll get to you in a minute. First, you reach across and get that sixgun outa leather with your left hand!'

It was awkward, as Dutch meant it to be, and Ringo half-turned away while easing his Colt out of the holster – his right hand inching around his back towards Cap's Colt rammed into his belt.

'*Dutch!*' yelled Mitch Cox reaching for his own gun. 'He's got a gun in his belt!'

Mitch's Colt exploded but the muzzle was still angled to the ground as Ringo's shot took him high in the chest spinning him into Chandler. Cox grabbed at the big rancher, inadvertently causing him to miss as he, too, fired at Ringo who was now diving headlong, triggering again.

Dutch Carnevan dropped his rifle as a bullet seared across his arm, leapt back into the brush, reaching for his own sixgun. Chandler and Cox had fallen in a tangle of limbs. The latter was groggy, but pushed free and awkwardly lifted his gun. His hand wavered, but he was determined to draw a bead on Ringo, now rolling into the brush. Kicking off a low, thick branch, Ringo brought Cap's smoking pistol around, dropping hammer.

Click! He swore softly, even as he threw the empty gun at Cox. Mitch fired, but his chest wound was getting to him now and he fell to his knees. Chandler rose up behind him, throwing down on Ringo. His bullet missed. Cox, weakening now, spread out on his face, though still raised his head and struggled to bring his Colt around.

Ringo dived for his own sixgun which he had dropped earlier as an added diversion to throw Carnevan's attention. Chandler fired again as Ringo slid under a bush, snatched for his gun, got it, but it wasn't a firm grip.

'He's . . . mine!' grated Cox with an effort, and triggered. Tough to the end, he didn't seem aware he was dying. But his aim was way off, although Ringo fell prone instinctively, firing two fast shots. Cox shuddered and the bullets' strike threw him on to his side. He flopped back on his face, nerveless fingers releasing his hold on his Colt. Even as he fell, Ringo fired again and Carey Chandler jerked, staggering. He did a brief wild dance, trying to keep his balance, but went down, crashing over a bush, moaning.

Ringo clawed dust and grit from his eyes, looked around for Dutch. He couldn't see him but heard him moving through the bushes to his left and ahead. As he searched for him, Ringo reloaded, ejecting the empty shells by feel and replacing them in the hot chambers with fresh loads from the belt loops.

As he snapped the cylinder closed, he heard a horse whinny and then the clatter of hoofs. He smashed his way into the clearing, almost stepping on Mitch Cox's hand. Chandler was struggling to get free of the bush where he had sprawled and Ringo clipped him with his gun barrel as he ran past.

He saw Dutch riding through the brush, crouched low, but not as low as Ringo expected. Then he saw why: the man had thrown the unconscious Jinx McMillan across his horse and was holding him in front of him. Ringo held his fire, gripped his right wrist with his left hand, steadying it as he sighted along the Colt's short barrel.

He knew from experience revolvers were notoriously inaccurate at any range much over a few yards but he tried to line up the blade sight on the racing horse as Dutch cunningly weaved it this way and that, smashing a path through the thick brush.

He held his breath, started to lift his hand from the hammer spur – then jumped and stumbled, his shot going wild, as a bullet buzzed past his head. Down on one knee, he twisted his body fast, Colt rising.

'I'll put a bullet through you if you don't drop that gun!'

Ringo blinked. Dale McMillan sat astride a foam-streaked chunky-looking black with bad-looking eyes. She was pointing a smoking carbine straight at him.

'Dutch Carnevan is getting away with your brother!' Ringo snapped.

'I know! That's why I stopped you from shooting! You might have hit Jinx!'

'I'd've brought down Dutch's mount!'

'And Jinx could've died in the fall, been crushed if the horse rolled on him!'

Ringo swore under his breath, let the sixgun sag, then rammed it hard into his holster. 'Well, it don't matter now. He's out of sight in those rocks and by the time I can get after him he'll have a lead it'll take me a week to make up!' Then added bitterly, '*Muchas gracias, señorita!*'

'To hell with you, Ringo! D'you think I'd risk my brother's life just because some trigger-happy drifter wants to take a potshot that could kill him?'

He shook his head, sighing, keeping his thoughts to himself, then started back up the slope. Her carbine muzzle followed his every movement. 'Cap! Cap, are you OK?'

The girl started as Cap Tyrell said in a gasping voice from slightly behind her and to one side, 'I got her covered, Ringo. Don't really want to shoot her but . . . you go ahead and do what you want to. She won't . . . interfere.'

Dale was pale now, seeing the old man swaying on his feet, fresh blood streaked across his cheek and dirty neck, the rifle he held, weaving wildly. 'Careful!' she snapped.

'Hell, yeah. I won't . . . won't. . . .'

Then he collapsed. Ringo rushed forward, the girl leaping out of the saddle swiftly, also running towards Cap. Ringo reached him first, dropped to one knee, seeing the bright, thin blood on the crumpled, dirty collar. He pulled the old shirt away from the skin and sat back on his hams, looking up at the girl as she arrived.

'It's not a bullet wound. He must've caught his face and neck on a broken branch or a rock. He's weak from fever. . . .'

She looked at him sharply – and he struck out swiftly with his left hand, snatching the carbine from her. She gasped, startled and stumbled in an effort to keep her balance.

'Give me that!' Her small gloved hand reached for the weapon, but he yanked it out of reach.

'I'll keep it for now. You're bossier than ever with a gun in your hand.'

She blinked, started to retort, stopped, anger narrowing her eyes. 'Who d'you think you're talking to?'

'I know who I'm talking to and I know I don't give a damn. Cap's more important to me than you.'

He swiftly worked the lever of the carbine, the shells ejecting and glinting in the sun. Then he tossed the gun into the brush and swept his Colt from the holster. Startled, she reared back, lost balance, sitting down hard. 'What're you—?'

But he aimed the gun past her and she turned her head quickly, saw Chandler groggily trying to get to his feet. He was covered in dust and leaves and twigs, his hard face marked with thin ribbons of blood from scratches inflicted by the bush he had fallen into. There was blood on his upper right arm, oozing through the dusty fingers of his left hand as he gripped the wound. His eyes seemed a little out of focus as he glanced towards Ringo.

'You're hell on two feet, mister! Dutch hates your guts and was always itching to square with you, but he never said you were this damn dangerous!'

'Dutch always holds back a little of whatever he figures will be to his own advantage.' Ringo nodded towards the man's arm. 'Bone broke?'

'Too numb to tell, but I don't think so. I can still wiggle my fingers.'

The girl was bent over Cap who was coming round again, coughing, making rasping, whistling sounds in his throat. 'How's he doing?'

'It's a nasty cut in his neck – I think it might require stitches.' She looked at Ringo, frowning slightly at his obvious concern. 'Is he kin of yours?'

He shook his head. 'Just an old man I met.'

'There's got to be more to it than that. The way you look out for him.'

Ringo shrugged. 'He pulled me out of a flooded river – thought you knew.'

'Maybe I did. That would account for some of your actions, I guess. I think maybe I understand a little better now. But maybe I still don't quite understand you, Ringo. Not that it matters I suppose. I'd still put Jinx first if I had to do it again.'

'I savvy that. It's a chore we still have to do, too – getting Jinx back.' He turned to Chandler, prying his fingers loose to look at the arm wound. 'Bone looks to be OK. We'll bind the wound and that'll stop the bleeding.'

Chandler watched silently, his heavy features unnaturally pale, as Ringo fetched rags from his saddle-bags and the girl washed Cap's face and gave him a drink from her canteen. 'Mebbe I can help with . . . Jinx.'

'You won't be able to do much fighting with your gun arm out of commission,' Ringo told him quietly. 'We know where Dutch is headed, anyway – Handy's place, isn't it?'

Holding his gaze to Ringo's face, Chandler nodded slowly. 'Make a good pair, Dutch and Handy. You know he's a kind of unofficial Indian agent? Handy, I mean.'

'I've heard whispers,' Dale said, still working over Cap. 'He's been in trouble for selling whiskey to the Indians.' Dale glanced at Ringo. 'I think the neck'll be all right after all. If I can wrap a bandage around firmly enough so it doesn't choke him.'

'Handy sells 'em more than firewater,' Chandler said suddenly, getting their attention. 'Dutch is dabblin' in some gun-runnin', wants to bring the guns to my place and have me pass 'em along to Handy.' He shook his head. 'Don't set right with me. My folks was massacred by Injuns. I still have my mother and sisters' scalps back at my spread to remind me – as if I need reminding.'

Ringo saw the compassion come into Dale's eyes, but she was quick to cover it. 'No one I know would pick you for a man of sentiment, Carey.'

He gave her a crooked smile. 'I know I'm a rough-cut. Had to make my own way since I was a kid. Finally found the spread I'd always wanted. An' was stupid enough to take a loan from Dutch Carnevan. I jumped in like a kid at a candy bar when he offered.'

'Now you know why,' Ringo said softly.

The big rancher nodded, grim-faced now. 'Yeah. He aimed to use my place for runnin' his guns all along. With me and Handy, he had an easy way in to the reservation.'

'And you do like he says or he forecloses on your ranch, right?'

'That's about the size of it. And just to make sure I toed the line, he planted that damn Mitch Cox on me. Night and day, I couldn't make a damn move without him. Hell, he even slept in the same room as me! Glad you nailed him, Ringo. I was aimin' to do it myself while there was a little lead flyin' around but you saved me the trouble.'

He grunted as Ringo tied-off the crude bandage.

'Arm's not gonna be much good to you for quite a while.'

'I'll manage. I figure you'll save me the trouble of havin' to worry about Dutch for much longer?' He arched his eyebrows but Ringo regarded him in blank silence. 'I can help some – I know a short cut to Handy's. Dutch'll still get there ahead of you but you take the trail I tell you about and he sure as hell won't be expectin' to see you so soon.'

'Can you draw us a map?' the girl asked, and saw the startled look on Ringo's face. 'You don't think I'm going to abandon my kid brother, surely!'

'I'll get him away if it's possible.'

'You see? *If*! I'm not satisfied with *if*! There has to be a way and I'm going along to find it – while you're worrying about *if* or *what* or *when*!'

Chandler almost smiled. 'I think you got company, whether you want it or not, Ringo!'

'He's got me, too.' All eyes turned as Cap Tyrell made his raspy announcment, struggling to sit up. 'I'm not passing up my chance at the Bosun even if you have to carry me in on your back!'

CHAPTER 11

WHIP HAND

Reed Handy disliked untidiness and grime in any man. He was always dressed neatly, though his clothes, washed and pressed, might well be some months old, even repaired in places, but clean. So his appearance was good enough for him to go most places. He insisted that anyone working for him dressed to his standard and shaved regularly – not necessarily every day, depending on how heavy the beard – and kept himself reasonably clean.

Work clothes were to be changed before supper-time – any man who thought he needn't bother, usually found himself sitting on the floor with a throbbing jaw and an empty belly. And kicked out to boot.

'Just because we live way to hell out here away from town and other folk, it don't mean we have to live like Injuns!' Handy despised Indians, no matter what their tribe or standing. If they were Indian, they

141

were sub-human trash in Handy's view.

That was why he enjoyed exploiting them.

'If they're dumb – and they sure as hell are! – then take advantage of 'em! That's why they were put on earth, to bring pleasure and profit to those smart enough to see the chance and take it.'

Despite his loudly stated hatred for anything Indian Handy was hypocritical when it came to taking his own pleasure with some golden-skinned maid. Mind, she had to be properly bathed and scented first: all part of the ritual before he took her to his bed.

He had built himself a profitable little empire way out here in the back-blocks. He only employed a few men. Often some were transients: stopping over on their way to a better chance at freedom in the nearby territory – all arranged, at a price, by Handy. He made his own laws, giving himself the powers of a god – life and death, seldom lenient, often brutal.

Now, lounging in the shade of his brush-roofed galleria at the front of his ranch house, smoking, he was amiable enough. There was a bottle of genuine Kentucky bourbon to hand – none of the belly-burning rotgut he peddled to the tribes. Insects droned in the heated air, their humming relaxing him.

Drowsily, he let his thoughts wander, wondering if that little Indian bitch he had seen last time at the camp would be available when he took in the first load of guns. He better push Dutch to get the delivery organized. She must be about twelve now, wouldn't remain untouched for much longer.

'Reed!' A rough voice intruded on his reverie and

he stirred, a growl deep inside him at the interruption. 'Someone comin' in – looks like he's bringin' a body with him.'

The words brought Handy back to reality with a snap. He thrust to his feet and grasped the porch rail, squinting into the sunlit yard: a tallish man, just under six feet, but well-muscled and formed. He was aware of the weight of the Colt at his hip as he looked beyond the sweaty, dusty cowhand sitting a mount in the yard, to where the man pointed.

The rider the cowhand was pointing to was not much more than a blur at this distance. 'Recognize him?' he asked, using a hand to shade his eyes.

'By the size of him, I'd guess it's Dutch Carnevan,' the cowhand said. 'Totin' someone over his saddle.'

Even as the cowboy finished speaking there came the sound of a gunshot, followed by two more. 'What the hell's he shootin' at?'

'Just tryin' to get our attention, I reckon.'

'Then go lend a hand, for Chris'sake!'

As the man spurred away, Reed stepped back into the galleria's shade, picked up the bourbon bottle and drank straight from the neck.

Three other men had left their chores at the sounds of gunfire. He yelled at them to get back to work. 'Blackie's handlin' it,' he growled. 'Jed, you go see if he needs help. You two get on with your chores.'

There was no argument or hesitation: Reed Handy might have some fancy ideas about his crew's cleanliness and dress, but he was no swanky dandy from the East; there were men who had worked for him who were now cripples to attest to that.

'Who's your friend?' Handy asked, indicating Jinx McMillan's ragged, battered body hanging head down over Dutch's horse when the man rode up with Blackie and Jed.

For answer, Carnevan tipped the semi-conscious boy off and let him flop loosely to the dust, where he lay, groaning.

'Recognize him?' Dutch asked harshly, dismounted, and knocked aside the canteen that Blackie proffered. He pointed to the porch. 'Gimme some of what's in that bottle.'

The young boy was now staggering upright, wrists roped together. He was groggy and unsteady on his feet.

'Step up and have a snifter, Dutch. How come you brought *him* here?' he asked, gesturing.

Dutch quickly poured himself a glassful of good whiskey and downed it in three gulps, smacking his lips. 'Jinx? Well, it's a long story, Reed – might have to lubricate the tonsils a mite before it's told.'

Handy nodded, tight-lipped now.

While Jinx was dragged off to the root cellar, Dutch told his story. Handy called to Blackie now down at the corrals, unsaddling. 'Get a fresh mount and go up to Snake Pass. Tell Buck to watch out for riders. If he sees anyone, he's to come back in pronto without alertin' 'em.' Blackie waved and Handy turned to Dutch. 'You bringin' me trouble?'

'Well, this Ringo's one hell of a shooter, Reed. But I reckon we can use the kid to pull him into line.'

'How far behind is he?'

Dutch shrugged. 'No idea, but he *will* come. And he could have company – including Dale McMillan.'

Handy's eyebrows arched. 'Yeah? Well, that ain't so bad – I could get excited over her, I reckon.'

'You better start thinkin' with your head instead of your pecker if you're coming in on this gun-tradin' deal.'

Handy knew Carnevan's reputation: had, in fact, modelled his own behaviour along Carnevan's lines, adding a few touches of his own. He was wary, but also resentful – this was his place and Dutch, nor anyone else, was going to come in here and order him around. Or criticize.

'You just worry about getting the guns,' he told Dutch stiffly. 'I'll handle my end – 'fact, already started.'

Carnevan frowned, lighting a cigarette and looking sharply at Handy. 'You gettin' guns from someone else?'

Reed Handy smiled, pleased that he had rattled the other man. 'No, no. Just got it in mind to make damn sure the Injuns'll do what we want, when we want it. I got a man I brought in specially to give 'em something to think about. Come inside and meet him before you wash-up . . . interestin' feller. A limey – sailed all round the world. And he's got somethin' that's guaranteed to get *any* man's attention.'

Dutch managed to get in one more swig of bourbon before following Handy into the house. 'This the one they call the Bosun?'

'Heard of him, have you?'

145

'Got some kinda fancy whip that can cut a man to pieces?'

'Yeah, cat o' nine tails, it's called. I figure just one Injun needs to get scratched up by that cat and we got 'em eatin' outa our hands. It'll terrify 'em.' He laughed suddenly. 'Hell! They could even be scared *white*!'

'It could work against us, too.'

Handy stopped, frowning. 'How?'

'You know how touchy Injuns are about their pride and their spirit. Whippin' any man strips him of a helluva lot more'n his flesh. You do that to one of them and, by hell, pretty soon you're gonna have an Apache in your lap – and it won't be no twelve-year-old maiden.'

Handy thought about it. He was both uneasy and angry, because Dutch could be right. *Shame one Indian, you shamed the whole damn tribe and bought yourself a parcel of trouble.* It was a touchy business messing with their spirit world. But it didn't sit well, having Dutch shoot holes in his plans. 'You got a better idea?' he challenged.

'Sure. Bring in the chief and the medicine man, couple of others, an' show 'em what could happen. Only use a white man.' He jerked a thumb over his shoulder. 'We got us a spare one in your root cellar. If they won't come here, have Bosun flog Jinx and take him up, let 'em see what we're willin' to do to one of our own – they'll begin to wonder just how far we'll go with them.'

Handy's man Buck, watching the twisting Snake

146

Pass, literally didn't know what hit him.

He was clutching his rifle, half erect behind his boulder, trying to see that swift, blurred movement again. Out there, at the edge of the scraggly timber – *something* moved, back in the dappled shadows. Might've been a bird flitting through a patch of sunlight, though he had the impression it was bigger than that.

Buck shifted position, straining to see. *There it was again! Judas Priest! It was a woman, on foot and—*

That was all Buck remembered. Something crashed into the back of his skull, crushing his hat, and he toppled forward, the rifle clattering.

Ringo stood over the unconscious man, holstered his Colt and took off his hat, waving it in a sweeping arc. Dale, watching from the timber, waved back and a couple of minutes later, she reappeared, mounted, followed by Cap, slumped in his saddle. Ringo's hunch that the old ex-prisoner might not make it through this deal was stronger than ever.

He should've insisted Cap go back with Carey Chandler, but it was hard to deny the oldster his chance at the Bosun. He had a damn good reason for wanting to square things with that scum, and if he was going to die anyway, he would feel better knowing the score had finally been settled.

But that was just one more worry.

Ringo reached for Buck's canteen standing in the shade of a rock, took a swig and poured some of the water over the groaning man. Blood from a cut in his scalp ran down the side of his face and Ringo propped him in a sitting position, poured more

147

water over him and shook him by the shoulder.

'Come on! Snap out of it!' Ringo's hand batted Buck back and forth across the face and the man blinked. Then his eyes widened as he looked down the bore of Ringo's Colt, a few inches in front of his face. 'Time for a little talk, feller. If you're smart, you won't waste a minute.'

Buck swallowed and nodded, unable to take his eyes off the muzzle of the sixgun.

'Wh-what you wanna know?'

They left Buck trussed like a turkey in the shade. He would be able to work himself loose in time and when he did, if he had any sense, he would clear this neck of the woods for keeps.

'Might come in to back up Handy,' Cap warned in his wheezy voice.

'I don't think he'll push his luck, Cap. You did good as our decoy, Dale, by the way.'

'So you finally noticed!' The girl was nervous, worried about Jinx. 'I was scared when you didn't signal right away and I had to run across a second time.' There was a hint of accusation in her words.

'He didn't know what he'd seen for a while. Gave him a few moments to keep his attention off me as I climbed into his hidey-hole.'

'He could've shot me!'

Ringo's cool gaze brought her up straighter in the saddle. 'You're here now. Unhurt. Don't be so damn tetchy.'

'*I'm* tetchy! Why you're—'

'Folks, we are running out of cover,' Cap broke in,

ending the terse warning with a rumbling cough. 'Best try to spot this root cellar where they're keeping Jinx.'

The trees had thinned and the brush was low here, skinny-branched, not offering much cover. They held back and scanned the ranch yard. Two men were trying to hang one side of the large barn door. Another worked over the rusted pump, replacing the main washer, looked like. They recognized the sorrel Dutch had been riding, nibbling at a hay bale near the corral, but unsaddled.

Then they saw three men on the porch. Dale pointed out Handy, Ringo recognized Carnevan, of course, and Cap, sounding as if he had a bad taste in his mouth said, 'And that snake with legs is Bosun Bates himself. Don't look much, does he? For the mean, miserable bastard he is.'

From here, Bates appeared to Ringo like a small-ish man, maybe in his forties. His face looked craggy and deeply tanned under an old mariner's cap. He was standing and Ringo reckoned he would be no more than five-seven, broad of shoulder, though, and with a strange impression of one arm being bigger than the other. He mentioned this last to Cap who snorted.

'It's had a helluva lot more use than his left arm. The right one's for swinging the cat. And he's been doing that for years.'

Dale gave an involuntary shudder. 'What an evil man!'

'You were a sailor on one of the old limey man-o'-war ships, you lived with the threat of the cat-o'-nine tails every minute of every day. You didn't dare even look hard at an officer or it was "Seize that man up to the gratings and give him twenty-four lashes!" '

'That – that's horrible!'

'Tough old days, and they made a tough breed of men, those limey sailors,' Ringo told her. 'Met one once – in fact, he was my father's half-brother, and he spun me some salty old yarns when I was just a shaver. Name of Norton Coe.'

Ringo watched Cap as he said it, but the old man began to cough and then Dale gasped, 'Look! There's the root cellar! And – and they're bringing Jinx out!'

Coming hard on what Ringo had just been saying, it was like a smack across the face to the girl: two men held Jinx between them. He was struggling and one time deliberately went limp, his feet dragging as they took his weight. One of the men, with shoulder-length yellow hair, clouted him across the side of the head. His hands were bound and they dragged him towards the corral fence where the man with yellow hair cut his bonds while the other man, bigger, his lantern jaw smudged with heavy blue stubble, held Jinx against the rails by a knee rammed into his back.

Jinx tried to make a fight of it but he was only an immature youth against two full-grown, hard-muscled men. Yellowhair's name was Chet: he pushed Jinx's already gravel-scarred face hard into the top rail. Dale made a small sound of protest and started to move, but Ringo took her arm, shook his head. Although she stopped, he felt her body tense, heard her sharp breathing.

'Oh, my God!' she hissed, as they tied Jinx's arms over the corral rail.

Then, their attention having been on the boy, they were surpised to see Bosun Bates strolling across from the *galleria*, a red baize bag in one hand, a crooked, anticipatory smile on his craggy face. Handy and Dutch Carnevan leaned on the rails, both smoking, Handy also holding a glass of whiskey.

It was clear what was going to happen to Jinx, even before Bates opened the red cloth bag, dropped it to the ground and shook the lumpy item he had taken from it. Ringo tensed as the nine knotted thongs spilled away from the thick handle. Bosun whipped them around his head and they heard the faint whistling sound even this far away. Then he drew them longingly and lovingly through his fingers.

He turned and looked towards the porch.

'Whenever you're ready, Bosun,' Reed Handy called and Dutch moved down the steps so as to get a better view. 'Just a warm-up before we take him to the Injun camp.'

Dale wheeled towards Ringo, eyes wild. 'We can't let this happen!'

He nodded, counting the odds, hand already drawing his Colt. Then they both ducked instinctively as Cap's rifle fired between them and Bosun Bates was driven forward by the bullet, stumbling to his knees, head and shoulders going between the lower rails. One arm was hooked over the lodge-pole and the cat-o'-nine tails sagged from his hand, but his fingers closed convulsively around the handle.

Chet and the other man sprang away from Jinx

who was sagging against his bonds, turning his head, trying to see what was happening.

Dutch Carnevan had his gun out, spinning towards the brush that barely hid Cap and his companions. Handy came bounding down the steps, his Colt blasting, calling to the men working on the barn door. They were already taking cover inside the barn: let Handy take care of the trouble.

Ringo dragged Dale to the ground and fired at Chet down by the corrals. The bullet sliced long splinters from the corral and the man stumbled away, clawing at his face. Ringo shot him and he fell. The other man triggered blindly and began to run, ducking between the rails, trying to catch one of the wheeling horses – it was every man for himself here, that was plain.

Cap stood, another cartridge in the rifle's breech as he coolly sighted on Bosun who was trying to push away from the corrals. The rifle fired and Bates's leg kicked out from under him. He sprawled, crying out. He dropped the cat and, face contorted with pain, strained to reach it with clawed fingers.

Cap calmly put a bullet through that quivering right hand and Bosun screamed as the bones shattered and the surge of unendurable pain made his small body jump and shudder.

Then Captain Ethan Tyrell jerked and went down in a tangle of limbs.

Ringo was already moving forward, bursting out of the brush now, taking the outlaws by surprise, so he did not see that Cap was hit. The girl's rifle was cracking and the man chasing a horse in the corral stopped in mid-stride and collided with the nubbing post before spilling to the ground.

Carnevan saw Ringo coming and he turned to run towards the barn but the men in there fired at him, making him veer away: they wanted no part of Ringo.

Dutch threw himself down, elbows scraping across the gravel as he tried to draw a bead on the running Ringo. Handy crouched and in something of a panic began fanning his Colt's hammer. The barrel jumped and threw the bullets all over the yard.

Ringo dived for the ground, shoulder-rolled, coming up on one knee. Handy turned and ran for the porch, flinging himself headlong on to it, rolling in and kicking over the table and one chair.

Dutch Carnevan leapt up and made a run for the corner of the building. Ringo fired at him, saw his lead kick dust from the porch corner and then Handy lifted above the rails, a rifle in his hands. Ringo dropped flat again, rolled onto his back and fired across his body. The bullet took Handy in the head, snapping it back, lifting him to his toes. He toppled forward over the rails and before he hit the ground Ringo was up and running, holstering his empty Colt, snatching up Handy's rifle.

Dale called a warning and he spun, half-crouched, rifle butt braced into his hip. The two men in the barn were making a run for it, both shooting at Ringo now. The rifle blasted in a volley of rapid shots and one man went down, skidding on his face before rolling on to his side and lying still. The other stumbled and yelled, throwing his Colt away from him.

' 'Nough! Chris'sakes, I've . . . had enough!'

'When I say so!' Ringo gritted as he hurdled the man and smashed the butt across his head as he did so.

He sprinted around the side of the house, saw Dutch struggling to get into the saddle of a grey horse that was nervous with all the guns hammering around it. He saw Ringo coming, hurled himself at the rifle and scabbard on the saddle. He threw his full weight on it and the rawhide tie-thongs snapped. He fell, rolled under the horse, gripping the rifle by the stock and flinging out his right arm so that the scabbard flew away from the weapon.

Teeth bared, Dutch levered and fired hastily. He was still partly under the frightened grey and the horse reared. A hoof thudded down on Dutch's leg. He yelled, cursing, crawled away, leg dragging, swinging the rifle around again.

He glimpsed Ringo, bent over, framed by the grey's heaving belly, as he thrust his rifle forward and triggered one-handed. The grey lurched away, knocking Ringo off his feet, but it was hot lead that flung Dutch a yard along the ground.

He stopped, lying on one side, eyelids drooping, mouth filling with blood as he tried to curse his old enemy. Scarlet spilled over his chin as he fell forward.

Ears ringing, dazed by the glancing blow from the grey, Ringo straightened, still holding Handy's rifle. Someone was riding hell for leather away on the other side of the corrals but he didn't bother trying to bring him down. Dale was at Jinx's side, untying the bonds holding him to the corral rails. He was trying to grin, bloody and dirty.

Bosun Bates was sprawled under the bottom rail now, holding his shattered hand to his chest, pain-filled eyes staring longingly at the cat-o'-nine tails, now half-trampled into the ground.

Then he saw Cap Tyrell limping and weaving his way across the yard, a hand clapped to his chest. Ringo sprinted towards the old man, caught him as his legs gave way. He started to lay him down gently, but Cap shook his head, pointed at Bates.

'Lemme see . . . him . . . die.' His wheeze changed to a cough and Ringo looked down at the sticky blood on his own hand where he held Cap around the chest. He swung the old man's legs up and carried him in his arms to within a few feet of where Bates lay, moaning sickly. But the sound stopped when he saw Cap, his eyes widening, as Ringo set him on the ground.

'You!'

'M-me, Bosun!' gasped Cap. 'Told you I'd settle with you . . . one day.'

'Take it easy, Cap,' Ringo said. 'He's not going anywhere.'

As Dale came over, helping Jinx, Bates squinted at Ringo, looking ghastly, fighting to stay conscious.

'You call him Cap?' Ringo nodded slowly and Bates added, 'Captain – Tyrell?'

'You ought to know.'

Bates surprised him by managing a sardonic laugh. 'That I . . . oughta . . . an' that ain't Tyrell: that's Jackson Scully, Tyrell's cellmate. . . .'

The effort was too much for the Bosun and he

sagged back, the intense pain making his senses reel.

But Ringo and Dale and even the dazed and injured Jinx, were all looking at the old man they knew as Cap.

Ringo said nothing, waiting for the oldster's breathing to ease. 'For nearly twenty years we shared a cell or barracks, Cap an' me. We knew everything there was to know about each other. Tried to stay . . . sane by talking about our . . . pasts . . . families, troubles – you know. . . .'

'Take it easy, Cap – or is it Jackson?'

'Keep it at Cap – it's a good name an' he was a good friend. But this son of a bitch – killed him!'

With weakening effort he managed to land a kick on the semi-conscious Bates's wounded leg, bringing a gurgling cry of agony from the man. They waited while Cap regained enough energy to continue.

'Said once the Bosun done me a favour an' didn't know it – well, it was this: both Cap an' me were caught trying to dig a tunnel outa that hell they called a jail so the warden ordered us to be flogged – by him.'

He tried to spit but didn't have enough saliva. 'I was lucky – my back healed OK. Cap's turned septic – blood poisonin'. Warden didn't want him dying in his jail so he transferred us out to another prison, locked in a box car by ourselves, no food, no water, nothing. Cap died on the way. Before he did he told me . . . told me. . . .'

'To switch identities?' prompted Ringo and Cap nodded.

'People at the other end wouldn't know who was

who – I took Cap's papers and left mine on him. See, he was due for release in a few weeks. He'd already done five years when they put me in prison. I got twenty-five years for hittin' an officer for mistreating a horse – I wasn't even in the army! I ran a livery in Fort Whipple. Officer banged his head on a rock and died. His friends made sure I got twenty-five years in hell. So, I figured if I could save five years jailtime by switchin' identities—'

'Anyone would've done the same thing, Cap,' Dale said quietly. 'It was a desperate situation and you did what you had to.'

He tried to smile at her but only managed a faint nod. 'I swore on Cap's body I'd find the warden and Bosun an' kill 'em both. Got the warden way up in Laramie and then I heard the Bosun had finally been fired and was in this area.' He rolled his eyes towards Ringo. 'Don't think I would've made it this far if it hadn't been for you – *amigo.*'

'I sure wouldn't've if you hadn't been on the island when the river flooded.'

'Needed that gold – as you know – to track down Bates.'

Ringo was silently studying the oldster now, then spoke quietly. 'One thing you might like to know: I mentioned my father's half-brother a little while back. It was a lie. I never knew my father. Never knew Norton Coe, but I wanted to see if the name meant something to you – it should've. I had just a few doubts about you, Cap.'

Cap was fighting hard to keep his thoughts together, frowned and then nodded. 'Yeah, Coe! Of

157

course, the lieutenant who was Cap's second – he was killed in Denver.'

'Yeah. And his widow remembered that when he was serving under Captain Tyrell, and she needed hospital treatment in St Louis and they had no money, Cap paid their bills and they'd never had a chance to repay him. She knew when the real Cap was to be released and she asked me to try to find him, bring him back to her small farm outside of Houston.'

'Why – you?'

'I was roustabouting in the district, building her a drying shed for her crops, when there was some trouble with a couple of deserters and I sorted things out for her.'

'With your gun?' Dale asked, but there was no disapproval in her tone. He nodded curtly.

'Well, thank her for the thought,' Cap said. 'Why din' you tell me before?'

'Wasn't sure who you said you were. Just a hunch, I guess, but you about had me convinced you were Tyrell when this trouble with Carnevan and Bates came up. . . .'

Cap shifted his fading gaze towards the Bosun and suddenly dragged Ringo's pistol from his holster. Before anyone could stop him, he fired it point blank into Bates's chest. The Bosun slammed back violently and the derringer he had worked out of his pocket with his bloody, though fully-functioning left hand fell half under his shuddering body.

'That's it now.' Cap fell back, no strength left to hold on to the smoking Colt. No strength to live –

almost. He swivelled his glazing eyes towards Ringo. 'Been good knowing you . . . *amigo*. . . .'

Ringo took the wavering hand in his, squeezed gently. 'Wish I hadn't doubted you, Cap. Widow Coe would have taken to you.'

Cap smiled faintly as he closed his eyes for the last time. Dale brushed at her moist eyes and Jinx said a trifle huskily, 'Seemed like a nice old feller.'

Ringo stood, reloading his gun automatically before holstering it. 'He kept his promise to Tyrell, squared the debt.' He looked around the yard, clearing now of drifting gunsmoke, the bodies and wounded becoming more discernible.

'We'll put 'em in the barn before we leave.'

On the way out of Snake Pass they found where Buck had rubbed through his bonds on a sharp rock but no sign of the man himself. Jinx ranged alongside Ringo on the dun he had picked up at Handy's.

'I gotta know somethin', Ringo.' The man looked at him, waiting. 'How come a . . . a man like you run out on Hondo when he needed back up? I mean, all that money sittin' in the express office an' just him left to guard it!'

Ringo didn't answer right away, then said quietly, 'Hondo never told me about the payroll.'

Jinx looked his disbelief openly. Dale, on Ringo's other side, frowned, waiting. 'Why wouldn't he tell you?' demanded Jinx sceptically. 'You were his deputy!'

'Temporary only, Jinx. He tried to keep the payroll secret. Didn't want anyone knowing. Someone knew,

159

obviously, but I didn't – not till I got back to town with the drunk decoy.'

After a while Jinx said, 'Then you set about puttin' things to rights. Only it was too late for Hondo.'

Ringo didn't bother to answer and Jinx looked past him to Dale. 'You believe him, Sis?'

'Yes, I do, Jinx. Hondo was always secretive. I don't know all about Ringo, but I've seen enough to know he's basically a decent man.' She turned to Ringo then. 'What'll you do now?'

'See Cap buried decent. Then go and report to Widow Coe.'

'After. . . ?'

He looked at her steadily. 'You could ride with me – as far as El Paso, anyway.'

'I thought the widow lived in Houston.'

'Yeah, but there's a monument in El Paso I think you'd be interested in. Jinx, too.'

'The one they built to honour Pa! Yeah! I'll come!' Jinx looked at Dale, waiting for an argument but they were almost out of the valley before she spoke.

'Perhaps. We could talk it over when we get back to the ranch.'

'Sure, grood idea,' Ringo agreed.